Viva

The Morelville Mysteries – Book 5

Prequel to the Morelville Cozies

Anne Hagan

To my mother and grandmothers

PUBLISHED BY:
Jug Run Press, USA
Copyright © 2015

https://annehaganauthor.com/

All rights reserved: No part of this publication may be replicated, redistributed or given away in any form or by any electronic or mechanical means including information storage and retrieval systems without prior written consent of the author or the publisher except by a reviewer, who may quote brief passages for review.

This is a work of fiction. Names, characters, places and incidents are products of the author's imagination or are actual places used in an entirely fictitious manner and are not to be construed as real. Any resemblance to actual events, organizations, or persons, living or deceased, is entirely coincidental.

Contents

CHAPTER 1: The Morning After 1

CHAPTER 2: The Smokies 11

CHAPTER 3: Gone 17

CHAPTER 4: Cabin Fever 21

CHAPTER 5: Lost 29

CHAPTER 6: Bullets and Casings 37

CHAPTER 7: Found 47

CHAPTER 8: MYOB 55

CHAPTER 9: Coffee Klatch 61

CHAPTER 10: Lifted 69

CHAPTER 11: PI Moms 75

CHAPTER 12: Positive ID 89

CHAPTER 13: The Sordid Side 93

CHAPTER 14: On the Road 97

CHAPTER 15: Manicures and Truth 101

CHAPTER 16: Home Sweet Home? 109

CHAPTER 17: Report! 115

CHAPTER 18: Bereaved? 121

CHAPTER 19: Family Fun Day 135

CHAPTER 20: Boo Boo.. 149

CHAPTER 21: Trash or Treasure 163

CHAPTER 22: Ah Ha Moments 169

CHAPTER 23: A Haunting We Will Go.. 173

CHAPTER 24: Seized... 179

CHAPTER 25: Denouement 189

About the Author 205

Also Written by the Author.. 207

CHAPTER 1

The Morning After

Sunday Morning, October 12th, 2014

"Good morning beautiful."

Dana stretched on the bed next to me but then she pulled a pillow that had strayed down between us up and half way across her face. "Turn off the sun," she groaned. "I'm not ready to get up."

"We don't really have a choice, babe. We have house guests, a mess to clean up at the farm and, well, there's the matter of a murder investigation I need to gear back up on."

Dana flung the pillow toward her feet and sat up on one elbow to look at me but then she dropped her head and ran a hand through her long hair. "That really happened, didn't it? I didn't dream it?"

"Yes, it really happened. Now I have to figure out what to do about it."

Dana looked worried, "Mel…our…our honeymoon…"

I knew what she was thinking because I felt the same. We've had a tough go of it these past couple of months, I thought to myself.

I looked at my wife, "I'll figure something out babe. We'll leave today, I promise." I just couldn't disappoint her. *She needs the time away. We both do.*

I showered quickly and then tiptoed into the living room. Nevil Harper Jr. was curled up in a ball in a sleeping bag on the floor. He was sound asleep. Chloe Rossi's giant Chihuahua, Lady, was curled up in the middle of the camp cot Chloe had slept on for the night but she wasn't in the room. I scratched my head and wandered toward the kitchen of our newly acquired home.

I found Dana's mom there measuring coffee out of a can she must have spirited away from the wedding reception we'd shared with my twin and her new husband Lance yesterday and transferring it to a new looking coffee maker that I didn't even know we had.

"Good morning Mel. I hope you don't mind; I opened one of our wedding gifts to you and Dana. I just can't get the day started without coffee."

"Oh, um, no problem." I nodded. I didn't have the heart to tell her I'm not a coffee fan myself. I got a glass of water instead and took a gulp just as she spoke again.

"That boy slept like the dead last night."

Trying not to spew water everywhere, I thought to myself, *you don't know the half of it!*

"What's his real story?"

"Pardon?"

"Oh, come on. Last night you told me he had family troubles and he needed a place to stay for the night. I know there's more to it than that."

"A little more. He's a, uh, witness to a case I'm working on."

She raised her eyebrows, "He's not in any danger is he?"

"No, and he's not *a danger* either, if that's what you're thinking."

I don't suppose you can tell me anything else?"

"No ma'am. Sorry."

"You're just like my boy Vince! You cops are all alike, I swear. I'm an old woman!" She elbowed me gently, "Don't you know I need a little bit of excitement in my life?"

"You're hardly old Mrs. Rossi."

"Mel, *please*, calling me 'Mrs. Rossi'. That makes me feel even older. Just call me Chloe or call me mama like everyone else does."

I just smiled and turned to dig in the fridge.

"Are you hungry? I can make you some breakfast, if you like?"

"No need to," I waved a hand toward the gaping open appliance. "We have all of these leftovers from the reception and there's a ton more out at the farm. We'll be gone all week so we really should eat up some of this stuff and haul the rest back out there. I don't know what we were thinking."

"About what?" Dana loped into the room, fresh from her own shower.

Chloe spoke before I had a chance to answer her myself, "Forget those leftovers. I promised your mom I'd stay the night and be out there to help clean up today. I'll take those back out to her myself. As for you two, you're just to be on your way after I send you off fat and happy with my homemade beef stroganoff."

"Ooooh," was Dana's only response.

Chloe smiled at her daughter, it's been a long time hasn't it?"

"Yes mama, it has."

I grabbed an oversized bowl of fruit salad and spooned some into another bowl. "I can live with that but if we really are going to get on the road this afternoon, I have to figure out what to do with my charge that's still in there sleeping and get my guys back geared back up on the investigation."

Dana simply nodded. I headed upstairs to where we'd decided to set up my office.

Our house was mostly unfurnished. We'd moved my bedroom suite and the desk and chair from my den over from the house I'd shared with Kris and her children when we took possession of our this one right next door and Dana had gone out and bought what kitchen and comfort items we needed to get by on for a week. We'd spent the week since we took possession of the home focusing on preparing for my twin's wedding rather than on furnishing and decorating the house. Dana was looking forward to jumping into that with a vengeance when we returned from our honeymoon.

* * *

Mama Rossi

"I didn't see sour cream in your dairy case. Do you have any?"

"Yes ma'am, in the back. I'll get you some; big or small?"

"Two large, please. I need one for stroganoff."

The man moved toward the back of the store while a woman took her time to ring up my other purchases. When she finished, she eyed me up and down with open curiosity.

"You know I'm not from around here but you think you've seen me before, don't you?"

The storekeeper seemed taken aback, "Are you some kind of mind reader?"

"No dear, it's written all over your face." I smiled, "I'm Chloe Rossi. I'm pretty sure we met briefly yesterday at the wedding for Kris and Lance."

"Oh, that's it!" Recognition dawned on her face, "I'm Sheila Ford. You must be a friend or family to Lance Miller then?"

"No, no. I said 'Rossi'. Dana Rossi is my daughter. She married Kris Crane's…well, *Miller's* sister, that wonderful peach of a girl, Mel."

"Ohhhh. *Now* I remember." The slight tint of a blush dusted Sheila's cheeks. Words spilled out in a rush, "We all just love Mel around here. She's the Sheriff you know. Well, of course you know. You'd know that…"

I reached out a hand and patted her arm gently, "Relax. I'm aware their relationship is more than a little unconventional for most folks around here. Really though, those two are so in love, who could ever deny them that? They only have eyes for each other."

"Yes, of course." Shelia leaned out over the counter and peered down the main aisle of her two aisle store. "Just where is Terry? I swear that man will be late to his own funeral! How long could it possibly take to fetch two containers of sour cream?" She stepped from behind the counter and marched off down the aisle toward the storeroom. She swung open the double hinged door and bellowed out Terry's name.

I started digging in my purse for my wallet and,

preoccupied, startled at the unexpected yell. I turned in time to see Sheila step through the door into the back area. As it swung closed again behind I heard her exclaim, "This is a fine mess you've made!"

Moments later, she emerged alone with the two requested containers.

"My apologies. Terry seems to have wandered off. There's a slimy mess back there where he must have dropped two of these and he's gone, probably in search of the mop while forgetting all about you waiting."

* * *

Mel

Once I settled in to work, I was thankful Dana had the cable company come out as soon as we took possession of the house. We hadn't purchased our own televisions yet, but we did have digital phone service and internet in the God forsaken no man's land that we lived in where, even on a good day, cell service was spotty.

After booting up my laptop and scanning through my email quickly, I spent the rest of the morning on and off the phone and computer trying to coordinate a renewed investigation into the death of Olivia Stiers based on Nevil Harper Junior's statements to me during the reception. Shane Harding, my only detective right now, was on his way over to pick Jr. up and take him into the station for a formal interview and a sworn statement. He'd handle the investigation from there, until I returned.

Nevil Junior wasn't a danger to anyone; I really felt that in my gut. I just couldn't lock the kid up but he couldn't go home either if he really did suspect his own father of the murder of his girlfriend.

After spending a few minutes thinking about what would work best for the 18 year old that had grown up far too fast the past couple of months, I dialed the Zanesville Toyota dealership where he'd been working before he disappeared. The service department was closed and the service manager wasn't in on a Sunday, but I was convincing enough with my urgent and authoritative tone to work an emergency number for him out of the woman at the front desk.

He answered his phone with a question in his voice, "Eric Graham?"

"Mr. Graham, Sheriff Crane. My apologies for disturbing you on a Sunday."

"No problem; what can I do for you Sheriff?"

"You had a mechanic working for you until a couple of months or so ago, Nevil Harper Jr."

"Yes. Great mechanic, for such a young one. We've missed him with the foreign stuff. Heard he got himself into some trouble though."

"He's not in any trouble himself Mr. Graham. Please understand, I can't go into any of the details but Nevil may have information about a case I'm working on. My department is working with him on that."

"Do you think I know anything about what he's talking to you about?"

"No sir, not at all. The reason I actually called is, well, I need to find a place for him to stay for a little while and, well, maybe…"

He interrupted me, "And maybe get his job back?"

"He's a good kid. He needs a hand right now and he needs money."

"I know he's a good kid; a good kid and a damn fine mechanic. Tell you what, why don't you bring him over here?" He rattled off the address, "I like the boy and we have plenty of room. If he wants to stay for a few days or for a while, we can work something out and I can always use his hands back at the dealership."

* * *

Mama Rossi
1:00 PM Sunday Afternoon

I waved at Mel and Dana as I pulled out of their driveway. Little Lady and I were headed out to the farm to help with what was left of the after party clean-up. They were packing up Dana's car for their trip to Tennessee.

I'd told the girls I'd be back for my bag later and that I'd make sure everything was locked up for them before I headed home. I really had no intention of going home this week but they didn't need to know that.

The farm was on higher ground than the house in the village. My cell actually got reception there so, as soon as I was stopped in the driveway, I called my husband to fill him in.

"Marco, it's me. Did you get in alright last night?"

"Yeah, no problems. It's only a two hour drive. You on your way?"

"No dear. I told you, I was going to stay out here and help out today. The girls just pulled out a few minutes ago. I'm back out at the farm now."

"So you'll be home sometime tonight then?"

"That's what I wanted to talk to you about."

"What are you up to?" His tone was accusing.

"Nothing like what you're thinking. They just moved into that house is all and it needs a lot of work…you know, cleaning and dusting and sorting and putting away; that sort of thing. I think I'm going to stay and do all of that and surprise them when they come home next weekend."

"Do you think that's a good idea?"

"How could they possibly object to a helping hand?"

CHAPTER 2

The Smokies

Mel
Sunday Evening, October 12th, 2014

I worked the key in the lock as I talked to Dana back over my right shoulder, "I got the recommendation for the rental agency from Terry Ford over at the store. I found this cabin online, through them. I hope it's a nice…" The handle turned and I stood gaping, speechless, at a beautiful wood and dark stone kitchen.

Dana nudged me forward to step in herself and look around. "This is nice but you ain't seen nothin' yet, I'm sure."

My spirits deflated, I knew Dana had been to the Smokies before. Coming here was her suggestion because she thought I'd enjoy it. From her statement, I figured she'd been in this cabin before. "I'll just get the rest of the stuff out of the car."

"Don't you want to look around first? I'm going to!"

"You mean, you haven't stayed in this cabin before?"

"Babe, don't be silly. Do you have any idea how many rental cabins there are dotted all over the Smokey Mountains?"

At my blank expression, she answered her own question, "Thousands. Lots of them are quite nice and, it appears, this is one of them."

We walked through the kitchen to the hardwood of the living room with its vaulted ceiling and sky high windows. We could see that outside a set of double doors was a deck and a hot tub, all with a beautiful view of the mountains.

Stepping out on the deck, we both took a look around. The cabin was perched on a hillside that rose to our left toward a ridgeline and fell away below us. A neighboring cabin on the left side as I faced outward was almost completely shielded from view by a row of thick pines. I hadn't seen any vehicles or activity there when we pulled up. The hot tub was on that side of the deck with a lattice screen behind it, despite the trees that shielded it from the neighbor's view.

Looking off the right side, back down the hill we'd driven up, we realized the closest neighboring cabin in that direction was several acres away with lots of trees dotting the unimproved lots in between. A grill was situated at that end of the deck. *We'll have plenty of privacy for any time we spend out here*, I thought to myself.

Dana looked at me, "We're about seven miles out of Gatlinburg. There's tons to do on the strip we drove down through Sevierville, Pigeon Forge and then Gatlinburg so this isn't very convenient to it," she waved her hand around, "but the cabins are a lot more plentiful and closer together there too; more people."

"This is nice. I like having a little seclusion and, compared to what we're used to, seven miles to civilization isn't all that far."

Dana grinned at that and nodded. "Let's go upstairs and check out the bedroom." She turned on her heel and headed inside. I followed like a lovesick puppy.

Viva Mama Rossi!

We climbed gleaming wood stairs to an enclosed loft style master with a massive, thick king sized bed sitting on the far wall facing what would have been toward the downhill slope, had there been a window on that side. Regardless, the room was so well appointed, I felt my jaw drop again. I went over and tested the bed. It was heaven. "We have *got* to get one of these!

"It would fit in our room back home nicely since Larry and Karen remodeled and expanded it," Dana replied.

I patted the bed beside me.

"Nope. Not yet. There's a bit more to see and we do have to get the car unloaded before it gets too dark. Bears can be a problem."

"Bears?"

She wasn't listening. Instead, she inspected the Jacuzzi tub a few steps to the right of the bed as she faced it and then opened the bathroom door alongside the Jacuzzi and peered in. Her smile as she turned back to face me said it all.

I got up and moved to the left of the bed toward double doors that led out to the balcony. When I walked out, I realized I was standing over the front of the cabin with the car just down below me in the little pull off from the road. Across the roadway that continued uphill to my right as I faced it, another hill also rose into a knoll. A copse of several trees stood tall at the top with a heavier wood line, just visible, farther back. There were no cabins visible at all on the steep hill on the opposite side of the road. With any luck, we wouldn't have neighbors all week in the cabin next door. I shuddered at the quiet and the seclusion of it all.

Dana took a small sip of her champagne then carefully set the flute down on the edge of the hot tub. I looked on as she sunk a little deeper into the bubbling water, relaxing after our long drive and the subsequent hauling in of the stuff we'd packed for the week. The champagne had been her little honeymoon surprise for us.

Her eyes closed and she allowed her head to loll to one side. I half rose and moved slowly to hover over her, being careful to keep my feet in the same position they'd been in and not give away my intent too soon. As I lowered my body to hers, I whispered, "Happy Birthday Dana; I love you." Her eyes flew open as I pressed myself to her gently.

"Mel, we agreed we weren't going to do anything this year, given the weddings, and receptions, and the house…"

I pressed my finger to her lips, "Shh." Removing it, I kissed her gently. "I didn't *do* anything special but I did at least want to say it to you, to acknowledge it." Slipping onto the bench beside her and gathering her wet form into my arms, I cradled her and nuzzled her neck.

"I didn't even let my own mother do anything for me today babe, and I know it was killing her."

"Oh, so you think the whole stroganoff thing was just a spur of the moment decision for her in our barely functional kitchen?"

Dana narrowed her eyes and peered into mine, "What are you saying?"

"Baby, she brought her own pans…"

My beloved tapped me lightly on the nose and then threatened, "You so owe me Mel Crane!"

"Hmm, what shall I pay?" I wiggled my eyebrows

suggestively as I tightened my grip just a little around her back and across her legs. My right hand slowly rubbed the outside of her thigh suggestively as we snuggled just a bit deeper into the water.

"I'll have to think about that."

"Oh really? I could just turn you over my knee and give you 35 good swats!"

"Go ahead and try it; I dare you!"

We tussled in the water for several seconds, her smaller form holding its own with the added bit of buoyancy she was able to gain over my larger one but, in the end, I captured her and lowered my weight on her. I claimed her lips in victory.

The kiss was searing in the already hot water. I rolled onto a bench seat and hauled her back into my lap, my hand firmly on her behind. I began to rub it suggestively through the lycra of the suit she'd insisted on wearing, though we were miles from anyone's line of vision.

Dana moaned a little against my mouth and arched toward me. Leaving an arm around behind her to hold her, I move my hand from her backside up to her shoulder. I lowered the strap of her suit exposing her breast to me then cupped it gently.

In the warm water, even exposed to a bit of the cooling night air, her nipple didn't peak at first. I rolled it between my fingers then bent to pull it between my lips. At the touch it pebbled and Dana bucked in my lap.

Keeping her in my mouth, I slid my hand away and down her front, between her legs, under the still bubbling water. Nudging the suit aside, I ran a finger along her slit. It was slick with a wet heat that I didn't think was just from the rolling water. Pushing into her core, I finally knew that she was wet in the best way and more than ready for me.

I nipped at her nipple as I moved one finger slowly in and out of her then, lifting my head and capturing her lips and tongue in a sweet torture that she was more than willing to return, I pulled out, then pushed two fingers in.

Going gently at first, then building harder and faster, I had her bucking and splashing as she tried to cling to me at the same time. Her walls closed in finally in several spasms and then she stopped thrashing in the water and went limp against me.

CHAPTER 3

Gone

Mama Rossi
10:40 AM Monday Morning, October 13th, 2014
Morelville

Sheila Ford sat at the kitchen table nursing a cup of coffee. Her brother-in-law Steven Ford was in a chair adjacent to hers doing the same.

Treadway looked back and forth between the two people. They were adamant about filing a missing persons report, though Terry Ford had barely been gone 24 hours. "So you last saw him, you believe, just after 10:00 AM yesterday morning?" He made an annotation in his notebook.

"That's right," Sheila replied. "I normally go to Sunday school at 9:30 and then the church service starts at 10:30. Lacy, our helper, called in yesterday morning just after Terry started to open at 9:00 and said her son was sick and she couldn't be there. I went in to help Terry get everything opened up. A woman came in just after 10:00 asking for sour cream. Terry went to the back to get it and he never came back. When I went back to check on him, there was sour cream on the floor and he was gone. I missed church and then ended up waiting there all day for him. He left his cell phone on the back counter." Her tone was angry then it softened, "He hasn't been back to the store or home since."

Steven spoke up, "We were supposed to leave on a fishing trip first thing this morning; a three day trout derby up at the lake sponsored by the Sportsman's Club."

Joe Treadway looked skeptical, "A derby during the week?"

"That's right. It was for the 55 and older group of members; mostly retired. Terry's a little eccentric…hell, even downright odd at times but it's not like him to miss a fishing trip especially for a derby." Sheila nodded her agreement.

"Was there any sign of a struggle in the back of the store or out in the lot Mrs. Ford?"

"No. Not at all…other than the sour cream mess. The containers both burst open. I assumed he went looking for the mop and he realized he probably put it out back in the storage barn, out of the way, or even that he had brought home for some reason and he came back here after it."

"Would he have brought it here?" Treadway asked her.

She shrugged. Steven too made a look like 'who knows' towards the deputy. He was the one to speak, "I told you deputy, Terry was an odd one. I think, more than that, he was getting a little forgetful as he aged."

"That's true. So," Sheila asked, "what are you going to do to try and find him?"

"I have a few more questions first. You said there was no sign of struggle. How would Mr. Ford have left the store?"

"Oh, we both use a side door back by the coolers to come in and out before opening and after closing. He would have gone out that way and gotten into his truck."

"He drove there yesterday?"

"He does every day. It's only a quarter mile from the house to the store but he's a smoker and not big on exercise. He won't walk it; says he can't breath."

"Where's the truck now, ma'am?"

She shrugged again. "Probably wherever he is. Is there anything else, officer?"

"Deputy. He's a deputy," Steven Ford corrected his sister-in-law gently."

"Just one more thing; is anything missing that you're aware of."

"No. I don't think so. I mean, see for yourself, all his gear for this trip he's supposed to be on is right there by the front door. He was excited…packed it all up Saturday night before he went to bed."

Treadway looked at Steven, "Are you familiar with the gear the other Mr. Ford usually takes with him sir?"

Steven nodded, got up and walked toward the weekend bag, tackle box, waders and other assorted odds and ends. He glanced over it then turned back to Treadway, "Everything appears to be here except his favorite pole." He pointed to a case, "That's his spare, broken down in that case, but he never took his favorite pole apart."

CHAPTER 4

Cabin Fever

Mel
Monday Afternoon, October 13th, 2014
Gatlinburg, Tennessee

"That was quite a night last night and then, our brisk little hike around this morning..." Dana sighed, "I'm feeling every bit of 35 today, that's for sure."

"Hey, what's that supposed to mean?" I demanded. Dana knew I was already 35 myself. We'd kind of glossed right past the birthday I shared with my twin in July. Dana was recovering from a kidnapping incident at the time and I was in the midst of a murder investigation that involved the criminal activity of one of my own staff. Celebrating was the last thing on my mind, then.

"You know what I mean. Between my leg issues and a level of *other* activity I'm not, ahem, used too," she cleared her throat suggestively.

I tried to hid my grin but I failed miserably. Instead, I suggested, "It's a little warm outside yet today but maybe you ought to soak it out in the hot tub; you know, to limber up a little bit."

"Naw, too warm outside right now, you're right. It must

be 70 out there. But, maybe I'll just go upstairs and give that Jacuzzi tub a try."

"Hmm, naked this time?"

"Well, yes. It's a tub silly!" She swatted at me lightly.

"I may just have to come and make sure you're doing the whole soaking thing right."

"Great…you're the reason I need to soak in the first place," Dana tossed over her shoulder as she marched as smartly as she could muster toward the steps.

After about a half hour of waiting downstairs at loose ends, I couldn't take the thoughts running through my head anymore and I went upstairs to check on my wife. I found her still lounging in the tub as it bubbled gently from the jets. She was leaned back against the far end which was along the same wall as the head of the bed. Her eyes were closed but, from the lazy circles she was drawing with the foot she had raised partially out of the water, I knew she wasn't asleep.

I stepped into the space between the bed and the side of the tub where the water spigot was. "Dana, honey, your water's probably getting cold."

She half opened her eyes and looked at me. "It feels so good in here. I don't want to move."

I glanced at the clock on the nightstand beside the bed, between it and the tub. "It's almost…"

I'd been about to say 'noon' when I checked myself and stepped over to look at the stand a little more closely. I pointed at the edge closest to Dana, "What does that look like to you?"

"What does what look like?"

"That." I moved my finger back and forth a few inches over the trim lip of the bedside table.

She leaned over the side of the tub to get a good look, "It looks like grimy fingerprints."

"Close, but not quite. It's fingerprint dust that picked up some fingerprints."

"Ewww!" Dana screwed up her face, "Are you sure?"

"Positive. Someone's done a crappy job cleaning this place but, worse than that, it looks like a crime may have been committed here. The place must have been dusted but somebody was slacking on the job and missed lifting these."

Once Dana was dressed, we drove down the mountain to speak with the management company. We needed to check in with them anyway since we'd arrived after hours but now I was far more angry than pleased with the cabin and I wanted some answers.

Heidi, a cutesy 20 something supposed property manager with a little gold name tag met us at the counter. "How can I help y'all?"

I pulled out my ID because I knew she'd need it but I left my wallet open with my wallet badge prominently displayed. "I'm Melissa Crane. We got in yesterday after you were closed."

The young woman interrupted, "Oh right, the Mountain Hideaway cabin. Let me just pull up your paperwork right quick." With that, she stepped away from the counter and back to a desk across from a man only slightly older than her who was expounding on the features of various cabins to someone on the phone. I stood there tapping my foot impatiently as Dana waited silently next to me.

She pulled some papers out of a small stack after rummaging through another larger one first. When she returned to the counter, she handed them across to me. "That there's your rental contract. I just need to copy your ID, I need her name if she's staying there with you," she pointed toward Dana, "and I need your signature on page three."

Listen, Heidi, about the cabin…"

"It's a nice one isn't it? It's one of our most popular ones for honeymooners…and… for couples." She paused, looking between Dana and I again, a question in her eyes.

I didn't owe her any explanations so I didn't explain our relationship. She, however owed me an explanation and I wasn't about to let her interrupt again. "Heidi there's a problem with the cabin and an explanation is definitely in order." I looked at her pointedly. The man on the phone, likely catching my tone of voice, stopped talking and looked my way too.

The young manager swallowed hard while trying to maintain her smile then looked toward the man on the phone. He asked the person on the phone to hold for a moment and then stepped quickly up to the counter. "I'm Josh, the GM. Is there a problem?"

"Yes Josh, there is. The cabin we're renting hasn't been cleaned very well at all after an apparent crime or an alleged crime took place there, possibly very recently. I'd like a full explanation, please."

It was Josh's turn to smile nervously, "Oh." He paused, and seemed to be gathering his thoughts.

After several seconds of my own impatience, I prompted

him, "Was a crime committed there?"

He finally spoke, "Sort of, yes."

"Sort of?"

"Actually, it was an accident, see."

"An accident?"

A woman was staying in the cabin back in September, a uh, a few weeks ago. She was out on the front balcony where she caught a stray bullet or something from a hunter and she was killed."

"She was killed on the balcony by a hunter?"

"That's what the police determined."

"Was anyone charged?" Dana asked.

Heidi piped up in response, "I don't think they ever even found anybody who realized they did it."

I was dumbfounded, "So someone was supposedly hunting, God knows for what in *September*, kills a woman by mistake, never comes forward and no one knows a thing?" The two managers simply nodded.

"Well here's my question then, if it was an accident, why did they dust the cabin for fingerprints in the first place and leave powder residue on the furniture?"

Josh shrugged a slim shoulder and held up his hands in protest, "I can't answer that. Maybe they did all that before they determined her death was accidental."

"Let's back up a bit, okay? What was the victim's name?"

Josh pursed his lips.

Dana jumped in to assist, "Look guys, it's a matter of public record. You may as well tell us because we're going to find out anyway."

"Oh, alright," Josh gave in. "It was Patricia Dunkirk. She

was a regular that would come down from Ohio and stay in one or another of our cabins every couple of months or so."

My eyebrows rose involuntarily, "Ohio, you say?"

They nodded simultaneously.

"Why would anyone have been hunting in the area in September? I mean, what's in season in Tennessee then."

"Technically, nothing was then," Josh supplied, "but you can hunt coyote and wolves year round because they're a nuisance, what with killing off chickens and small house pets and such. That cabin's not far from the local sportsman's club. Some of their members were known to be out in the area hunting coyotes at that time. Cops figured one of them shot at a one and the bullet found her instead."

Heidi, found her voice, "I can get someone up there right away to give your cabin a thorough cleaning or, we have a couple of empty one bedroom cabins right now, we can, um, move you maybe," she looked to Josh for confirmation, "if you like."

Before I could speak, Dana nudged me with a foot below the counter and out of their view. "Neither will be necessary," she said. "We'll take care of it."

Once we were outside and out of earshot, I questioned my wife, "Dana are you sure? Why don't you at least want them to clean it?"

"Something isn't right Mel. I can feel it; don't you?"

I set my mouth and nodded at her. Once we'd climbed into her car, I admitted, "Yeah, I do too. My primary question is: why would the police dust for prints inside the cabin if they thought the shooting was an accident? Something inside had to originally trigger them to think it was murder.

We drove through Gatlinburg, through the park and down to the strip in Pigeon Forge, chatting about the 'how's' and 'what if's' as we went. Once we were seated in one of the many pancake houses that seemed to dot the strip and Dana had decent cell reception, she pulled out her smart phone and started searching on the name 'Patricia Dunkirk'. It didn't take her long to find something.

"The top result is from the Gatlinburg daily newspaper from the day after the shooting reporting that an Ohio woman, Patricia Dunkirk, was shot and killed on the balcony of any area cabin. The body was reported to police by an anonymous male caller. When police arrived at the scene, they found her lifeless, on the balcony wrapped in a towel and wearing a swimming suit that was wet. She had an apparent gunshot wound through the neck. No other persons were present in the area. The caller that reported her body had not come forward at press time. The Gatlinburg Police Department and the Sevier County Sheriff's Departments are investigating. They are asking anyone with any information to contact the county crime hotline or to come into either station to make a report."

Dana scrolled down a bit. "That's it for that article."

"There's no pool anywhere nearby," I said. "If she was in a swimming suit and wet, she was either in the hot tub downstairs at the back, which makes no sense unless she went upstairs to change and went to the balcony for some reason, or she was in a suit in the Jacuzzi, got out and went to the balcony."

"There's a whole déjà vu, statement…" Dana smiled and

went back to her search results but shook her head several times as she scanned through them. "Most of the reports are from the next day or a day or so after that. Nothing says much more than that." She paused as something seemed to catch her eye.

"Did you find something?"

"Yeah, a short mention in the same paper. About a week after she was shot, the Sevier County DA ruled Dunkirk's death 'Negligent Homicide,' a Class E felony in the State of Tennessee. Still no suspects though."

CHAPTER 5

Lost

7:30 AM Tuesday Morning, October 14th, 2014
Morelville

Joe Treadway looked from face to face at the group of volunteers assembled outside the Morelville General Store. He cleared his throat and, when all eyes focused on him, he began speaking, "Terry Ford was last seen, as far as we know, here in his store on Sunday morning at approximately 10:10. He left the store for reasons unknown in his blue, F-150 pick-up truck." Treadway reeled off the plate number for the truck.

"It does not appear that Mr. Ford at any time came back to the store or went back to his home. At this time, we do not suspect any foul play. Mr. Ford may be out there somewhere, injured and in need of assistance. Our job is to mount a search and rescue operation to find him and get him home safely."

He looked around, "I'm going to divide you into a few teams. Would those of you who know Mr. Ford, please raise your hands?"

Jesse Crane and several others in the gathered crowd raised their hands. Would you all please step over by the SUV to my right? Thank you."

Addressing the dozen or others left after 20 some people

stepped aside, he said, "We'll be teaming the rest of you up with a couple of the folks who know Mr. Ford and one of our officers. Thanks for coming out to help. Please stand fast while we get everything under way."

Jesse Crane was chatting with Steven Ford when Treadway moved over to their group to start breaking them down into teams. "Deputy?" he called to get his attention.

"Yes sir?"

"I'm Jesse Crane, in case you don't remember me, and this here's Terry's brother." Jesse jerked a finger toward Steven.

"We've met," Treadway supplied.

"We suspect he might have grabbed his favorite pole Deputy and headed to one of his honey holes to fish. Something may have happened. I know a few places he might have gone."

"Okay, great. That's a good start. I'll assign you two to Deputy Gates and you can go around with him to all the places you know of."

Gates stepped forward. Treadway reminded him to report anything they found back to him then he beckoned to the two men to follow him to his cruiser.

Jesse looked at the patrol car and clucked his tongue, "This ain't gonna work Deputy. We might just need four wheel drive for some of the places we're going. We better take my truck."

"Is that okay with you Mr. Crane?"

"Wouldn't have offered if it wasn't."

"Lead on then."

* * *

Viva Mama Rossi!

Mama Rossi
8:00 AM Tuesday Morning, October 14th, 2014
Morelville

My, my things sure kick off early out here in the country!
I looked over at the General Store as I passed by. There were people and police cruisers clustered about. Slowing my car, I turned off the state route by the only gas station in the little village my daughter was now calling home and then picked my way back around to the store.

Bypassing the deputies and the folks outside, I went into the store. I was surprised to find The main aisle shelving shoved back into the only other aisle and tables set up inside. Faye Crane and another woman were hovering about behind the counter, getting crockpots set up while Sheila Ford sat nearby, on a bench under one of the front windows, staring off into nowhere.

I hadn't expected to find Faye there. I'd never said anything to her during the party clean-up about staying on longer but, now was as good a time as any. Before I could frame my approach, she spoke first.

"Why Chloe, this is a surprise. I thought you were headed home last night." Her smile reached her eyes and I felt instantly at ease. She hadn't handled her daughter marrying mine very well but, the past few days, she'd been quite friendly toward me. Now that the official festivities were over, that seemed to be continuing.

"To be honest, I'd actually already decided to stay on and

sort of, how to explain it, help our girls out. My Dana's not completely mobile right now and your Mel is just so busy."

"Help out how dear?"

"Oh, you know, this and that. A lot of cleaning, a little organizing, maybe seeking out some – *a few* – furniture and décor items…"

"Do they know you're doing this?" Her eyes narrowed slightly as her overall look took on an air of suspicion mixed with curiosity.

"Um, not actually, no."

Faye's demeanor changed again, "Ooo, a surprise! I love the way you think!"

The other woman tried to squeeze by Faye with a wrapped tray of sandwich rolls. Faye excused herself to the woman and then turned back to me and said, "I apologize but I really should be helping. Those guys will all come back hungry here in a couple or three hours and we need to be ready."

"That's why I stopped. What's going on?"

The second woman stopped and stared at me, "You mean you haven't heard?" she asked.

Faye flipped a hand in her direction, "Oh Helen, she's not from around here. She's just here visiting." Lowering her voice and tipping her head toward Sheila, she told me, "Terry Ford is missing. He left the store Sunday and he's not been seen since."

I looked at Sheila and caught her attention, "The guy you were in here with on Sunday morning when I came in to buy the sour cream?"

"Her husband," Helen provided.

Sheila finally broke her silence, "That's right," she

looked me up and down, "you were the one that was here. He never came back after he dropped those sour creams you wanted." She started staring off into the distance again.

Faye leaned across the counter toward me and whispered, "She's got it in her head that he either took off or he's out there dead somewhere. Terry's brother convinced her they needed to mount a search and rescue effort so that's what's going on this mornin'."

I was shocked but I quickly gathered my wits and asked, "What can I do to help?"

Faye patted my wrist. "Nothing dear. We've got it under control in here and the searchers out there all know the county and, I dare say, Terry, pretty well. They'll find him and he's going to be just fine, just you wait and see." She raised her voice a little for Sheila's benefit and looked toward her on that last bit.

"You're sure?"

"Yes, of course. Now, tell me, what are you getting yourself into today with this plan of yours?"

I smiled, "I spent yesterday cleaning. They did a decent enough job when they moved in but, not like I do it."

Faye nodded knowingly.

"Between you and me, I've slept in their bedroom the last couple of nights since they don't have much furniture. They need some nice guest room and living room furniture but, that's just such a lovely old place…all of the gorgeous woodwork; I just think they'd love to have a few choice antique or vintage feel pieces to show it all off, don't you?"

"Oh my word, yes. You're right."

"I know my Dana's tastes but I'm not sure about Mel's…"

"Mel isn't picky dear. She tends toward things that will last, like her father. Old and antique for some things will do just fine for her but she likes her comfort too."

"It's too bad you can't come along with me. That would be fun *and*, you could keep me from making too many mistakes…Hopefully they find Mr. Ford soon and he's alive and well."

"I hope so too but, at least, I can give a couple of tips for now."

"I'm all ears. Tell me where I should go."

"Well, there are furniture stores in Zanesville, of course, and lots in Columbus too, if you want to go that far. There are Amish furniture makers dotted through the hills around here that you really should check out for wood pieces that will go well with the woodwork in the house and sit well with my daughter."

"How would I find them?"

"That's the problem; it's easier to show you than to tell you. Maybe, we can go out together tomorrow for that. In the meantime, you should head north toward the turnoff for Zanesville, just before you get there, on the left side of this road, there's a junk shop an old friend of Jesse's owns, Dale Walters; Dingy Dale we call him."

"Dingy Dale? That doesn't sound too promising."

"Oh, you might be surprised. You never know what you'll find in Dale's place and he's harmless, just a little cuckoo."

"What makes you say that?"

"He's, what's the word…'quirky', I guess, and he's always been full of odd ideas. Lately he's been making what he calls art out of what everyone else calls junk. No one around here buys the stuff of course, but his place is always chock full of all sorts of odds and ends."

"He usually opens around 9:00. By the time you're done there, Lucy Sharpe's antique shop will be open out on 146. Instead of turning left when you get to it to go into Zanesville, turn right and head toward Chandlersville. There's signs. Her shop's down about two miles on the right, before you get to the village. Sharpe's Antiques; you'll see it."

CHAPTER 6

Bullets and Casings

Mel
Tuesday Morning, October 14th, 2014
Gatlinburg, Tennessee

"You're liking that tub a lot…we have one at home now…our home, remember?"

Dana turned her head toward the bed where I was lounging, watching much of nothing on the TV. "Yes, I know, but at home, I don't get used and abused quite so much. You work all day at least five days a week."

I grinned, "You love it; you know it."

"Yes, but that's not the point. I have to recover from each round, see, and prepare for the next one."

"If you insist but, really, it seems like I'm doing most of the heavy lifting."

"Are you calling me fat now?"

Whoops! "No, no! That's not what I meant. Not at all." At her look, I continued, "I just meant that I do most of the, um, work…"

"Is that right Crane? Keep digging!"

"You're twisting what I'm saying all around."

"'Is that right' was a question."

"Not the way you said it, it wasn't." I grinned wide,

hoping to diffuse what I was picking up might not be so funny to her. When her look softened and she cracked a small sliver of a smile, I shifted my legs over the side of the bed and favored her with my most earnest expression, "Dana, honey, you're not fat at all. You're beautiful and I'm so blessed to have you in my life."

"Are you sucking up now?" She was trying to be serious but she couldn't keep the hint of a laugh out of her voice.

I played along, pretending to be hurt, "You're so suspicious! *No*, I'm not sucking up. I was being honest. Now, I'm being honest about something else, I'm starved. We've only tried one Smokey Mountain pancake house. There must be forty more of them out there to try."

Dana sighed, "I'm hungry too but I sure don't want to drive all the way into Pigeon Forge yet this morning. Let's look for one in Gatlinburg."

"I'll boot up the laptop, you get dressed."

"Yes ma'am!" Dana snapped off a salute from her reclined position in the tub.

I pulled my laptop from the case and fired it up. While I was doing that, Dana turned off the jets and released the drain on the tub. I watched as she stood carefully on the slick surface still draining of water and reached for her towel on a hook on the wall just behind and to the far end of the Jacuzzi tub, near the bathroom door. She started to rub and pat herself dry but, when she realized I was watching her instead of focusing on my own task, she laughed and turned her back to me. I liked that view too but Windows finally opening caught my attention and I turned my concentration to the screen.

"Now, what the hell!"

Dana's words were part question and part exclamation. My head shot back up and my eyes found her standing motionless in the middle of the tub, her back still turned to me staring at the wall behind the tub that divided the bedroom and bathroom. "What's wrong babe?"

"Come here and look at this." She pointed at the wall.

I stepped over to the edge of the Jacuzzi and leaned toward her. She moved aside slightly but pressed her finger to the wall just below something that was lodged into the thick, glazed pine paneling.

"Is that what I think it is?" She waited for me to respond.

"If you're thinking it's a bullet, then yeah, I think so."

I retrieved my cell phone and the small pocketknife I always carry from the desk where I'd dropped the contents of my pockets the night before. I grabbed a water cup too and, after stepping gingerly into the tub, I took a couple of quick photos and then I carefully pried out the bullet that was lodged completely into the wall and sunk about an eighth of an inch past the otherwise smooth surface. A small caliber, jacketed shell dropped into the cup.

Dana and I both peered intently at the hardly deformed round.

I was shaking with anger again. "Is everybody around here incompetent? First the cleaning crew and now the cops too?"

"Since it's a jacketed round, it must have passed through Patricia Dunkirk's neck Mel and ended up in here. That might explain the dusting powder on the nightstand."

"Or she was shot in here and somebody is covering

something up. This looks like a .22 shell. .22s just don't have that much range; you know that as well as I do."

Dana nodded.

"Stand there in front of where it was, facing me." She did as I asked.

Since I was still standing in the tub myself, I sized up what I was looking at from there, looked toward the balcony door, then I peered over the edge of the tub. "Okay, so if Dunkirk was standing in the tub, facing an *open balcony door*, when the round came through and it hit her in the neck, passed through and lodged in the wall, she was three, maybe four inches taller than you, even standing up here in the tub where you've got 2-3 more inches of height. If she were on the balcony or anywhere else in the room in the line of fire when it hit her, with the door open, then she was probably about your height and we have to account for the round coming in at a lower point like from a shorter shooter or from outside.

Dana stepped out of the tub and began getting dressed while I inspected the wall around the point of impact and below. I didn't find a trace of any sort of blood spatter which doesn't mean it wasn't there, *if* this was where Patricia Dunkirk took the fatal shot.

I inspected the woodwork on the wall. *This wood is pretty heavily polyurethane coated here to protect it from water damage. That would make it pretty easy to wipe down quickly and, of course, the tub would clean easily too.*

"What are you thinking, Mel?"

"Just that, since she was in a swimming suit – which is odd, granted – *and wet* when she was found and the bullet was here, she had to have died here," I pointed at the tub as I stepped out of it. "There's no evidence of blood there of course with all the easy to clean surfaces but, since the body was found on the balcony, there would have been blood transfer in the process of getting her out there."

"Why aren't you considering that she really could have died on the balcony after going out there in a swimming suit?"

"I'm just thinking about the caliber of the round…it's small…the range of such a pistol or rifle and the angle of the shot if the shooter was outside." I looked at my wife and shook my head.

"What? You're thinking something Melissa Crane; tell me what it is."

"It's really bugging me babe. I want to check the angles. Will you help?"

"I'm curious too. Go for it."

"Alright then. I'll go outside. You stand on the balcony to start with out in front of the door and leave it wide open."

I went downstairs and out the front door, turned and looked up at Dana whose feet were roughly 9 feet above my head.

"We can establish that if the shooter were outside, say a hunter, from anywhere this close the angle is all wrong." Dana just nodded. I stepped off about 16 feet to the edge of the parking pull off in front of the cabin then crossed the road and the opposite berm, calculating width in my head. "We're roughly 38 feet right here, at the base of this hill but we're not close to the angle of trajectory the bullet would have had to take."

Wheeling around, I started up the knoll. The slope went from gentle to steep pretty quickly leaving the distance still under a total of 25 yards by the time I reached the top. The copse of trees was thirty more yards behind me.

"From right here I have a clear view of you and the angle seems about right if you were a little taller. I simulated holding a rifle then a pistol."

Dana shot back, "Yes, but a *hunter* with a clear view wouldn't have taken the shot."

"Good point; hang on." I backed up to the copse of trees and realigned myself with Dana and the door. To take a shot at the right angle, I could still see her very clearly. No hunter, in his or her right mind, would have fired.

"Can you go and stand in the tub?" I yelled.

I stood my ground on the hilltop while she complied. I could see her less clearly now that she was 10-12 yards further distant and in the interior of the room but, unless I backed up to where the knoll dropped off just a little behind me, I could still see that I was shooting straight into a cabin. The angle of trajectory was only right from the edge of the hill or near the front of the clump of trees I was in. *No hunter took a shot from anywhere up here!*

Using a hunter's eye, I looked around me. There were no tracks in the dry earth now and, in reality, I was contemplating the events of a month prior. The trees still had the majority of their leaves now full of color but not yet ready to give way. Still, on the unused hillside, deadfall from storms and fall seasons past lay all around, mostly undisturbed, other than where I'd walked myself.

Peering closely at the ground, I began looking for signs

of other human traffic and I began edging leaves with my toes around the largest trees in the right sightline and just to either side of them where an ejected shell casing might have landed. I was about to give up when a tiny glint of metal caught my eye. Stepping to it, it was immediately apparent that it was a shell casing and for a small caliber bullet at that.

All around me were only leaves. I chose a large freshly fallen one and edged it under the cartridge. When the case was firmly in the middle of the leaf, I pulled the corners up around it and carried it down the hill with me like that, not touching it.

Dana stared into the cup where the shell casing I'd found now rested beside the bullet we'd dug out of the wall. She shook her head, "They sure could go together."

"Yeah, but there's no proving that unless there are matching fingerprints on both. You have to touch them somewhere to load them but that casing has been out in the elements."

She shifted gears, "So, you could see me in the tub?"

"Yes but it's not a shot anyone but someone bent on killing Patricia Dunkirk would have taken and, given that it's a soaking tub, what are the odds of her standing up right there and being framed in that doorway?"

"What are the odds of that door being open? There's a lot of 'ifs' here."

"True, but it's still too whacked to be accidental. Either the shooter was in here and intended to kill her or out there and got lucky. The shell casing I found may or may not be…"

Something flashed in my head and I picked up the cup to

look at the bullet again.

"What were you saying?"

I didn't even hear Dana's question. Tilting my head, I asked her instead, "Have you ever hunted?"

"Noooo, not personally. My dad and my brother Vince do. Why?"

"I'm not familiar with the hunting regs in Tennessee but they're probably similar to Ohio. You can't hunt big game with a rifle, only a shotgun. You'd probably want a shotgun anyway to hunt coyote. You can use a .22 caliber rifle in Ohio for small game like birds, rabbits and nuisance animals like groundhogs and coon."

"Okay, where are you going with this?"

"That's just it Dana, a *seasoned hunter*, trying to help thin out the coyote problem wouldn't be out with a .22, *rifle or pistol*, and it's probably completely illegal here, *like it is in Ohio*, to hunt with full metal jacketed rounds. It's very dangerous and any licensed hunter would know that. The damn things pass right through stuff!"

Dana shuddered, "What a mess!"

We were both quite for a couple of minutes, thinking, then I got up and went upstairs. She followed.

I turned on all the lights in the room, opened the drapes to the only window and opened the balcony door next to it again. Starting at the balcony, I walked a slow line through the door, around the bed and then over to the tub, looking at the carpeting as I went.

"If Dunkirk was on the balcony when she was shot, someone intended to kill her. The problem with that scenario is, after impact with her, a .22 bullet would have been slowed and the trajectory changed even though it was a jacketed round that passed through."

"Agreed."

"If Dunkirk were anywhere in here, with a shooter inside or outside, there'd have been blood spatter."

"She had to have bled heavily from a neck shot…had to…"

"But there's no blood anywhere on the carpet. Not around the tub and not on the path to get the body outside. Granted, this could have been cleaned and it's likely that it was cleaned after she was shot but certainly, it hasn't been replaced. This carpet isn't new in the past month or so. It's been here a while."

CHAPTER 7

Found

Mama Rossi
Late Tuesday Morning, October 14th, 2014
Morelville

I found Dale Walters shop easily enough but I wouldn't have even noticed it or thought to stop there if Faye hadn't told me too. His building was a non-descript place covered in dust that came, no doubt, from the dusty, pitted parking area out in front of it. When I got up close to the door, I realized it was stenciled with a circular, 'Dale's Curios'. *Who knew?*

Stepping inside, I felt like I'd entered a different dimension. There were odd and unusual things and old, reclaimed things everywhere. They lined narrow aisles on the floor and they hung from the walls and ceiling. In every inch of space, it seemed, something was on display with only enough room for humans to pass and marvel at it all.

A gentleman about my age appeared from a narrow doorway near the back. "Good morning. Can I help you ma'am?"

"You must be Dale, I take it?"

The man didn't reply directly, he just tipped his head to the side and half nodded.

"I'm Chloe Rossi. Faye Crane told me I should stop here and take a look around."

The mention of Faye's name brought a smile to his face, "Ah Faye, sweetheart Faye. Such a lovely woman. So tell me, are you looking for anything in particular?" He spread his hands wide, taking in the eclectic mix of his shop.

"This is one of those, I'll know it when I see it type of stops, I guess you could say."

"Well, you're in the right place for that! Please, take a look around and, if you need any help, just holler."

As I wandered around, I came to realize that Dale's shop had more decorative pieces than furniture pieces but there were the odd few handmade chairs here and there. Much of what Faye had called junk were art pieces that were reasonably priced compared to what I'd have paid in the city for similar things, if I had been interested in them.

When I'd worked my way back to the front, Dale was standing at a counter near the door that I hadn't even realized was there when I came in. He looked at my empty hands and then my face. A look of what I took to be disappointment flashed across his own face but he plastered on a smile.

"I take it you didn't find anything to your liking?"

"Oh that's not it at all."

"It's not?"

"I liked several of the art pieces here, especially the ones that seem to be make out of odds and ends but that resemble something completely different than their materials."

His chest puffed out a little, "I make those myself. I call them the 'Sum of the Parts Collection'."

"They're amazing Dale."

He grinned wide but then cocked his lips to the side and looked me over at the same time as he pushed the glasses that were sliding down his nose back up. "No one from around here ever buys them. They think they're too expensive, too weird and that I'm crazy." He scratched his head and went on, "I am a little crazy but that's what lets me be creative, you know?"

"Let me tell you, I'm going to come back in here. I'm actually shopping to help decorate a house but I need furniture pieces first and then art and décor. I'll be back here for things to use for finishing touches, how about that?"

That seemed to please Dale because he beamed broadly. Handing me a postcard sized business card, he said, "I look forward to it. Take that along with you, why don't you, so you can keep my little piece of heaven in your mind's eye."

Fifteen minutes later I entered the entirely different, more organized, more refined world of Sharpe's Antiques. The place was clean and neat but at the same time arranged to be warm and inviting without the feeling of being engulfed in clutter or in the grime of age.

A woman, somewhat older than me, approached me as soon as I'd crossed the threshold. "Hello dear, I'm Lucy. How may I help you?"

"I'm Chloe Rossi; Faye Crane recommended your shop to me."

"Oh, I know who you are dear. I was at the reception for Kris and Lance and your Dana and Mel. Lovely party, just lovely."

"Yes, it was. Faye and the girls did a marvelous job

putting it all together. But now," I let out a tiny sigh, "the work begins. Mel and Dana just moved into their own house and, because Mel was living with Kris and her children, she only took what was specifically hers with her. My Dana has recently left a government position that had her living in hotels most of the time so they need *everything*."

"Of course they do! I'm glad you came here first."

I smiled to myself, at ease that I didn't have to jump to the defense of daughter and daughter in law.

"First things first though; how about a cup of tea?"

* * *

Tuesday Afternoon, October 14th, 2014
Near Morelville

"It's Gates; we've found him." The deputy un-keyed his mike and looked out again at the body of Terry Ford floating, facedown, in the pond before him.

Jesse and Steven both stood surveying the scene too. While Gates made arrangements to retrieve the body, they stood beside Jesse's truck, parked behind Ford's own missing pickup, and talked between them.

"Look," Jesse pointed toward the bank, "there's his pole right there." It was lying on the bank, a line out in the water with no bobber or other marker in sight. "Bet it's tangled out there somewhere." Steven Ford simply nodded.

Gates asked them, "Is this public or private property?"

"Belongs to Chuck Knox," Jesse said. "Him and Terry

go way back. Terry fishes here all the time. He takes bluegill; helps keep their numbers down for Chuck so they don't overrun the pond."

Within 15 minutes, Jesse and Steven were relegated to the confines of the truck while Mel's Deputies swarmed the scene. They watched as two deputies put on waders and went out in an inflatable raft to retrieve Terry's body from the middle of the still pond.

Once Terry was retrieved, having no other transportation back to his cruiser, Gates climbed back in the truck with the two men. Steven Ford began to quiz him. "So, what do you think Deputy?"

Gates was diplomatic, "Mr. Ford, I'm very sorry for your loss."

"I appreciate that but I need to know where we go from here. Who will investigate?"

"The Coroner will see to your brother sir if that's what you're asking."

"I'm asking about a murder investigation deputy. What's next?"

"There isn't going to be a murder investigation Mr. Ford."

"Why the hell not?" Jesse asked, jumping into the fray.

"There were absolutely no signs of foul play out there at all gentlemen; no tracks at all and no other signs that anyone else had been there. His line was snagged out in some reeds. It may have snagged and when he waded in to try and free it, he slipped, and…well, anyway, the Coroner is probably going to rule it an accidental drowning."

"Bull!" Jesse was angry now. "Do you know *anything*

about fishing Deputy?"

Gates admitted that he didn't fish.

"Well, we both do," Jesse turned his head and looked at Steven in the back seat, "and we can tell you that something stinks here." Steven nodded.

Gates, riding shotgun, looked at Jesse driving and then back at Steven too. "Tell me what you see that we don't see," he asked.

Jesse blew out a heavy breath, "Look Deputy, someone's been here; had to be. The ground's just too dry and firm right now for you to tell it but *we* know it." He tossed his head toward Steven Ford in the back."

The older Ford brother spoke up, "You can't fish without bait or tackle Deputy Gates. If he *was* fishing, where'd it go?"

"Yeah, and Terry wouldn't have gone in the water without putting on his waders. He sure wasn't wearing them and I didn't see them in the bed of his truck," Jesse added. "If the line was snagged, he would of just cut it." He glanced in the rearview mirror at Terry's brother for confirmation.

Steven Ford leaned forward between the two front seats, "His waders are probably still sitting by the door where he had them packed up for the trip we were supposed to leave for yesterday morning."

"His boots are probably there too, ain't they Steven?"

Terry's brother nodded.

Jesse continued, "Terry didn't have boots or waders. He was in his work clothes. He didn't even have his favorite fishing hat. All of that strikes me wrong."

* * *

Viva Mama Rossi!

"Chloe? It's Faye Crane. Listen, they found Terry. Jesse and I, we're both home now. When I went by the girls' house, I saw you out directing Lucy Sharpe's delivery guys. I'm just dying to know what you bought. Why don't you come on out to the farm for a nice dinner and a night out of that empty old house? Call me back as soon as you get this message."

CHAPTER 8

MYOB

Mel
Early Tuesday, Afternoon, October 14th, 2014
Gatlinburg, Tennessee

We were cooling our heels in a little visitors waiting area at the Sevier County Sheriff's Department. I wasn't happy about how long we'd been waiting. I was being polite but I'd expected a little professional courtesy here and I wasn't getting it.

Deputies came and went through the area Dana and I were sitting in, laughing and joking. After more than 40 minutes without so much as an acknowledgement that we were still there by the Deputy manning the inquiry window, I went back to it and stood there until he could be bothered to acknowledge my presence.

"Question ma'am?"

"I just wanted to let you know that we're still out here and we're still waiting to speak to your Sheriff or the investigating officer on the Patricia Dunkirk shooting."

"I'm aware of that Deputy…, what did you say your name was?"

"Crane; Sheriff Crane." I was trying hard to keep my voice even and my temper in check.

"It will be just a few more minutes *Sheriff*." His tone was condescending and I didn't believe him. All I could do though was nod and go back to my chair beside Dana. She just set her jaw and shook her head.

Another 15 minutes passed before we were finally called back only to be put in a sparse interview room.

Dana shuddered, "Bad vibes in here."

"Yeah, this is probably the last place *you* want to be after all you've been through. I can't imagine why they felt the need to put us in here."

"Simple," Dana said, "there's a two way and it's miked. They can listen to and see everything. Maybe they'll take what we have to say seriously."

The words were no sooner out of Dana's mouth than the partially closed door swung open and the portly Sheriff of Sevier County blustered in. "So sorry to keep you little ladies waiting. I hope it wasn't too long?"

Condescension seems to run through this department... I stood while Dana remained seated. "Sheriff Trainor," I said, reading his name tag, "I'm Sheriff Crane from Muskingum County, Ohio and this is my associate, Special Agent Rossi." I only felt a twinge of guilt using Dana's former title with the self-important man standing before me.

"Sit, sit please. Coffee? Tea perhaps?"

Dana spoke up, "No thank you Sheriff. We're here officially."

I sat back down. Trainor took a chair and turned it around to straddle it facing us like a thinner, fitter man might. "How can I 'officially' help you ladies?"

Already tired of his attitude, I just dived in and hoped to

get the meeting over with quickly. "Agent Rossi and I are in Tennessee on some personal business. We're staying in the Mountain Hideaway cabin just outside of Gatlinburg where Patricia Dunkirk was shot and killed last month."

"Ah, yes. The accidental shooting. So unfortunate."

"Your department did investigate?"

He eyed me warily but answered quickly, "Of course, of course. Wasn't much to it though. She stepped out on the balcony and caught a stray round from a hunter, poor thing." He pursed his lips and shook his head to emphasize his sympathy but his eyes held no sorrow and I wasn't buying his act.

"Did you find the bullet that struck her on the scene Sheriff or did the Coroner find it at autopsy?" His eyes darted right and he licked his lips before he answered me. I knew a lie was coming.

"I believe so, yes."

"You believe so or you did?"

"I don't rightly recall but, regardless, it's not a matter of public record and I shouldn't have said what I already have."

"I can hardly believe that you can't recall something that happened roughly a month ago and that you think I'm here just digging for information without something of value to add to your investigation."

Trainor stared at me but didn't respond.

Dana asked him, "Why do you believe a hunter killed Dunkirk?"

"Why, because that's the only plausible explanation, of course. She wasn't from around here. No one here had any reason to harm her however, there have been problems with coyotes in that area and the Sportsman's Club near there had a sort of a bounty on them running that weekend. Their members were out all over those hills. One of them probably took a shot and never even realized what happened. As I said, it's just so unfortunate." His look was smug.

"Patricia Dunkirk was supposedly standing on a balcony several feet off the ground. To hit her, a hunter would have had to have been aiming upward or have been out across from her on a hill on the opposite side of the street where he would have had an unobstructed view of her."

Trainor waved me off, "There are tree stands all over those woods, uh…"

""Sheriff Crane, and *no* Sheriff, a hunter in a tree stand would be aiming down, not up, besides, there are no tree stands in the thin copse of trees atop the knoll across from the cabin in the line of trajectory to hit Dunkirk."

Now his face reddened, "How on earth would you know what the line of trajectory was?"

I pulled two baggies out of my pants pocket and laid them on the table in front of me. "One of those is a full metal jacketed bullet that we dug out of the wall behind the Jacuzzi tub in the master bedroom in the cabin this morning. Before we dug it out, I took photos of it and its relative location. The other is a shell casing that would seem to fit that shell that I found on the opposite hillside a reasonable rifle or pistol eject distance from the line of sight. I understand that they may go together and they may not but, certainly, the bullet is damning evidence that someone was gunning for Dunkirk."

"So you're a bullet expert huh?"

Half standing and leaning across the table toward him, I

was indignant. "I'm a County Sheriff, a 12 year veteran of the department and I've been hunting since I was big enough to hold a gun." Dana grabbed a belt loop and started to haul me backward.

Trainor leaned back away from my advance and, after almost falling off the chair, remembered he had it turned backward.

"Okay, ladies, I admit, the bullet is a mite suspicious but the shell casing is entirely coincidental. It could have been there for years. Frankly, I'm writing all of this off to coincidence. It was a hunter because there is no other plausible explanation."

Exasperation seeping into her own voice, Dana implored him, "Sheriff Trainor, Why on earth would someone be hunting coyote *with a .22, with jacketed rounds* and aiming that high? Most hunters would use a shotgun for one thing and, I checked, you can't use jacketed rounds to hunt in Tennessee. It's illegal. I'm sure any hunter here would know that."

When she finished, Trainor leaned slightly forward in as much as leaning into the chair back would let him, "Tell you ladies what; I'll have one of my men look into it."

"He's the laziest, most condescending piece of shit I've come across in my law enforcement career!" I was venting once we were in the car and out of earshot but Dana seemed to be pre-occupied. When she didn't respond, I tapped her leg to get her attention.

"Sorry; just thinking."

"Penny for them…"

"I heard you Mel but I don't think it's laziness. I think it's more than that. The Sheriff, maybe his whole department, they're hiding something."

"Like what?"

"That, I don't know but they must have had a reason to dust the cabin for prints."

CHAPTER 9

Coffee Klatch

Mamma Rossi
Tuesday Evening, October 14th, 2014
Crane Family Farm, Morelville

"Terry was a tough nut to crack. Some liked him, some didn't," Jesse stated as he toyed with the food on his plate.

Faye shot me a look that told me the subject of Terry was off limits so I tried to change it. "Your message said you wanted to know what I'd bought at Sharpe's. You'll never believe the deal she gave me on a…"

Not normally so talkative, Jesse interrupted and just kept going, "I figure there'll be a funeral Friday or Saturday. That Sheila, she's just too distraught to decide anything right now. The arrangements probably won't be made until morning." He hung his head down and stared through the table.

I traded glances with Faye. We continued with dinner in an uneasy silence until Jesse abruptly pushed his plate away and stood.

"There's chores to finish and I'm wasting daylight." With that, he was out the door and headed toward the barn.

"He's sure taking this hard. Were he and Terry close?"

"Jesse was a year behind Terry and two years behind his

brother Steven in school but they all played football on the same high school team. Jesse was tight with him and with Terry's best friend Chuck Knox; even dated Chuck's sister for a while before we started going out."

"You two were high school sweethearts?"

Faye nodded, "Yes; married right after we graduated. By then Chuck and Terry were both married too. Steven went off to the Army – Vietnam - so he wasn't around much in those early days."

"The other men weren't drafted?"

"My Jesse is a sole surviving son. The Army wouldn't take him. Chuck eventually went but Terry had some sort of medical deferral." Faye cupped a hand beside her mouth, "Just between you and me, everybody always said Terry wasn't quite right in the head."

Faye slapped her own cheek, "Listen to me, speaking ill of the dead." She stood, "How about a little cake Chloe and some coffee to wash it down with?"

"Some of that amazing wedding cake that Hannah girl made?"

"Of course. I froze the top tiers for the kids for their first anniversaries but there's still a little of each cake left too."

"That was divine. Count me in."

While Faye poured coffee and dished up cake, I wondered aloud, "Why would Terry just leave the store the other day without a word? I mean, he was working. He goes to the back to fetch something and suddenly he forgets everything and goes fishing? It doesn't make any sense."

"Oh, I agree. Terry was a little eccentric, granted, but the whole thing is just too odd of a situation, even for him."

"You've said that twice now, that he's odd and eccentric. How so?"

Faye set a slice of cake down in front of me then returned to her own seat. "Well, let's see, it's just the sorts of things he does and the way he does them. He's been known to hunt a little out of season. That's against the law but he never seemed to care. He's been caught trespassing on the private property of older folks when he was out mushroom and ginseng hunting without getting their permission to do it. He'd just sweet talk them into taking a little of his mushroom haul or splitting the cash for the ginseng since they were no longer able to go out and get it for themselves. Who knows how much he's gathered that he's never been caught for. He always had plenty of money for those smelly Sweets he liked to smoke and for poker, I'll tell you that!"

"It seems like he had little regard for the law but that doesn't make him odd."

"Around here, folks would tend to disagree with you on that but there's more. He's something of a player, what I've heard called a serial monogamist."

"I thought he got married right after high school?"

"He did, but not to Sheila. She's his *fourth* wife. They've only been together a half dozen years or so. I'm not entirely sure he's been faithful this last year or so. Rumors have been flying."

From what she'd told me, I took Terry for a low level criminal and a cad. 'Odd' and 'eccentric' really didn't ring true for me and I was prepared to write the whole subject of him off when Faye interrupted my train of though.

"Jesse and Steven are convinced Terry was murdered."

I was shocked, "What?"

"They think someone killed Terry."

"I heard you the first time; what I want to know is why they think that?"

"Jesse and I talked a bit on the way back from the store this morning after the search. Him and Steven are dead set about it." She outlined the things the two men felt were unusual at the scene.

"It certainly does sound like there could be more there than meets the eye but don't you think Mel's men can figure all of that out?"

"According to Jesse, her crew was convinced to a man that it was a drowning case."

"They are professionals, Faye."

"Maybe so but if my Mel were here, things would be different. She'd listen to her father and look into it."

"Have you called Mel and let her know about Terry?"

"I've been debating that. He's known my girls all their lives…she'd probably be upset if I didn't at least tell her he's gone."

"You should probably call her, Faye."

Faye put down the coffee cup she was about to raise to her lips, "You're right." She rose and picked up a handset off the counter. A house phone still seemed to be commonplace out here I noted, while she dialed.

"Mel, it's mom. I'm so sorry to bother you on your honeymoon, but I have some news I think you should hear." She paused and listened very briefly.

"Honey, Terry Ford went missing on Sunday and they found him…your father and Steven found him…today, drowned in Chuck's pond."

I could hear Mel exclaim but I couldn't make out what she said. Faye spoke to her for a few moments and then put her on speaker phone.

"Mel, baby, I hate to say this but your dad and Steven both don't believe it was an accident. They both say somebody that had it in for Terry might have seen to it that he drown. Your officers aren't pursuing any kind of investigation."

Mel's voice came across the phone. I could tell she was in a car. "Did the coroner take his body mom?"

"Yes dear; your dad said he did."

"Okay then, Luke will do his thing and determine if there's any reason to investigate further. If he does think so, my men will handle. If not, there's not much I can do if my deputies didn't find anything at the scene to implicate anything other than an accident."

Without thinking that the girls didn't even know I was still in Morelville, I spoke up to put my two cents in, "Mel, just how much do you trust your Coroner?"

"Chloe? Is that you?"

Oops! "Err, yes?"

"What are you doing there?"

"It's a long story…I, uh…"

"Hang on Mom, Chloe." There was a brief pause at the other end of the line then Mel came back on, "Now *you two* are on speaker phone. We're in the car. Dana's driving."

"Hi baby! Are you having a good time?" I attempted to coo at her and distract her.

"Mama," Dana questioned, "What's going on? Why are you still there?"

"It was supposed to be a surprise dear but I guess I blew it."

Dana sounded leery, "A surprise, how?"

"I stayed on and I've scrubbed down your house for the two of you and organized your cupboards and closets."

Mel spoke, "Wow, Chloe that's awesome. Thank you!" Apparently speaking to Dana, she asked, "Isn't that awesome?"

"Yeah, it's awesome alright," Dana's voice dripped with suspicion. "What else Mama?"

I let out a breath slowly. I was found out and I knew it. I went for a flattering approach, "You two have such pretty woodwork in this house, it just begs for some nice things to go along with it is all."

"Oh my God, what did you buy Mama?"

Cringing at the fear in Dana's voice, I recoiled a bit but then I mustered a little confidence and I told her, throwing Faye under the bus too, "Faye recommended a lovely antique shop to me and the owner made me a wonderful deal on a gorgeous bedroom set that looks to die for in your guest room." Faye slapped my shoulder lightly.

Dana and Mel both spoke at once; Dana asking what else I'd purchased and Mel chastising her own mother for her role. I addressed Mel first, "Now, don't go getting mad at your mama Mel! I told her what I intended to do no matter what and she gave me advice to steer more toward things that would appeal to your tastes too and not just Dana's"

"What else did you buy, Mama?" Dana's tone was more forceful this time.

"Nothing yet dear, I swear."

"Yet?"

"Whoops, did I say that?"

"Yes."

"You've *only* been gone two days. I spent all of Monday cleaning and organizing. I got the set this morning and a mattress set and had it all delivered this afternoon; that's all."

"Chloe, that sounds expensive. You shouldn't be spending your money on us."

"I'm not poor dear."

"Melissa!" Faye cautioned.

Mel was immediately contrite, "I'm sorry; I didn't mean to offend you."

"No offense taken."

"What else do you intend to do Mother?" Dana was being formal now.

"Honestly, I planned to stay the week and surprise you with it all when you got home. Other than that poor, poor man's death, it's been a nice break away from the city, for me."

Mel's voice came across the line, "If you two will hang on just a minute, I need to ask Dana something." With that, there was silence. Faye and I just looked at each other. I sipped on the dregs of my coffee.

Finally sound came from the open line and Dana started talking, "Mama, we'd like for you to go ahead and stay for as long as you want to. We don't mind you continuing to do *some* shopping for our home but on our dime now, not yours." She told me where I could find the keys to the lock box where she kept a spare bank card.

"Okay, honey. I agree to that."

"Wait Mama Rossi," Mel said, "There's more. Mom? Are you still there?"

Faye's eyes grew wide, "Um…yes…"

"What are you doing this week?"

"Well, now that Terry's been found, just working around the house…at least until funeral arrangements are set."

"I want you to keep me posted on those but, in the meantime, *we* want you to go with Chloe."

CHAPTER 10

Lifted

Mel
Tuesday Afternoon, October 14th, 2014
Gatlinburg, Tennessee

"Are we going to live to regret that?"

Dana looked back across the table at me, rolled her eyes and shook her head. "You don't know my mom that well yet. Had we not said, 'go ahead', she would have continued right on as she had been. Hopefully your mom being involved will buffer some of that."

"I wouldn't count on it. You just gave those two free rein with your bank card."

Dana groaned low. "What a day we've already had…"

Our server brought our sweet teas. "Have ya'll decided?"

Dana, already familiar with the barbecue joint we were sitting in, in Gatlinburg, ordered herself the sampler platter with the house sauce on the side and a side of mac and cheese. She smacked her lips after ordering that last bit.

The college aged waiter turned to me, "For you ma'am?"

Trusting the instincts of my always hungry wife, I ordered the same. The young man smiled and took his leave.

"You won't be sorry babe. Bennett's is the best around here."

We chatted for just a few short minutes about what to do with the rest of our day but because our food was presented so quickly, we abandoned that conversation in short order and tucked in.

Dana finally lifted her head about half way through her lunch. "You know what bugs me about this whole mess?" she asked. "It's their indifference. A woman died for heaven's sake. *Someone* shot her. Because you can't figure out something right away or because she's not local, you just write it off? That just doesn't fly with me."

"I can't stop thinking about it either. The trouble is, there really isn't anything we can do about it, at least not till we get back to Ohio."

"What then?"

"Think about it, you said yourself, you thought the police here are hiding something. That may be true. That they're lazy may also be true though. She's from Ohio. She dies here by an unknown hand that probably wasn't a hunter. Maybe someone from back home wanted her dead and followed her down here to do it."

Dana half shrugged, "It's certainly possible."

"How's your lunch ladies?" I hadn't even noticed the server approaching the table.

"Just fine," I managed.

"Pardon me for interrupting but I couldn't help overhearing, were you two talking about that woman that was shot?"

Dana nodded but I didn't say anything.

"That was such a shame. They were good customers, used to come in a couple of nights a week or more because he really liked the brisket and she was a fan of our ribs."

"She was with someone when she died?" I asked him, trying not to sound over eager.

"Not that the papers said, no, but she was usually down here with a man for a weekend or a few days every month and, like I said, they'd eat dinner here a couple of times each time."

"Did you know them?" Dana asked.

"Personally? No, not outside the restaurant. I just know regulars when I see them and they were pretty regular."

"Do you know his name?" I asked him.

"Sorry, no. Had I known, I'd have told the police then." He took his leave to attend to another table.

"Funny," Dana said, I made him out to be a college kid picking up some extra hours before every place around here slows down for the dead of winter. Sure seems like he's been around."

"Not only that, his information was more helpful then maybe he even realizes. Patricia probably wasn't alone and the prints may very well have told the Sheriff's department who was with her had they bothered to finish lifting them."

Dana looked at me, her expression puzzled, "So, you'll do some digging then when we get home?"

"Yeah, but here's another thought: they haven't sent anybody by our cabin to clean again and it's doubtful they will before we leave. We need to try and lift those prints."

"How?"

"The old fashioned way, transparent tape."

We ran into a drugstore after lunch and got a small roll of

packing tape and some rubber gloves.

Looking at the prints, back at the cabin, I could see that they were angled as if someone had knelt on the floor between the stand and the Jacuzzi and reached out to touch it, maybe for stability on the way down to their knees or back up. They certainly were oddly located and positioned to be plausible for any other explanation.

As carefully as I could, I lifted the prints highlighted by the fingerprint powder and inspected my work. There was little residue no left on the stand and it appeared I'd gotten good transfer to the tape. *Local incompetence might just pay off yet*.

While Dana packed the tapes up for shipping, I called my old friend Izzy at the crime lab in Columbus and asked her for a favor. She agreed to let me overnight the print tapes to her so we headed back out to find a place to ship them from.

It was early evening by the time we were out and about again. The Gatlinburg post office was closed. We found a Pak Mail place that told us they'd send it out but that we'd missed the overnight pick-up. Izzy wouldn't get the prints until Thursday. I left her a message and then gave my wife the once over.

"It looks like we've done all we can do for now, babe. It's back to enjoying each other's company."

Dana smiled up at me, "I'm okay with that."

* * *

Viva Mama Rossi!

Wednesday Morning, October 15th, 2014

We woke to a cool morning drizzle in the Gatlinburg area but, after jumping on the laptop, Dana determined Cherokee North Carolina was experiencing a beautiful fall day. She packed us up and we headed out on a leisurely trip through the mountains and into North Carolina.

We enjoyed the great outdoors for a while and then, in the heat of the day, we packed it into another one of Mama Rossi's favorite casinos to take bus trips to, as Dana tells it, Harrah's Cherokee, and we lost as much money as we could stand to lose. Dana's past luck with handicapping pro baseball games didn't seem to extend to playing blackjack, video poker or slots. I didn't plan on letting her forget it.

CHAPTER 11

PI Moms

Mama Rossi
Wednesday Morning October 15th, 2014
Morelville

Faye picked me up at 9:00 sharp in Jesse's pick-up truck. I'm not fond of the things but she said it would be useful for anything we bought 'cash and carry'.

Since it was on our way out of Morelville, we stopped at Dale's shop first. I was excited this time. While Faye took her time moseying into the place, I burst through the front door to find Dingy Dale himself standing not ten feet in front of me.

"Good morning Chloe. I'm glad to see you made it back after all." He nodded to Faye who was finally crossing the threshold behind me.

"Now Dale, I told you I'd be back. I bought a lovely antique bedroom set yesterday and I saw just the piece in here to compliment it. I hope you still have it." I just barely caught Faye's look as she rolled her eyes.

Working my way around to where I'd seen the carved lamp base, I ran across an old dry sink in need of a little TLC. Looking around, I found Dale trailing semi-discreetly behind me. "Was this here yesterday? I don't remember seeing it."

The quirky shop owner half smirked. "Good eye Chloe; no it wasn't. I got it in late yesterday afternoon. I just knocked the cobwebs off a little and put it on out here while I decide what I want to do with it."

I called Faye over, "Wouldn't this be just perfect in that corner of the kitchen just inside the door? It's just a useless little area there right now."

Faye, index finger to her lips, considered it. "I think you're right but it needs some work." She looked at Dale, "What are you asking for it, as is?"

"It's an antique you know."

"Don't try to kid a kidder Dale. You know you trash picked this somewhere. If we take it just like that, what do you want for it?"

He scratched his head, "Mmm, gimme a hundred and it's yours."

I didn't think his price was bad for something that was oak, obviously vintage, and only in need of some stain and a little hardware. Faye had other ideas though.

"What were you thinking about doing to it?" she asked him.

"Obviously, it needs cleaned well and a nice coat of oak stain then I gotta fix that pull."

"Tell you what, you do that stuff and we'll give you your hundred." Faye looked at me and I nodded but I still felt like we were stealing it from the man.

"You got yourself a deal." Dale stuck out his hand and I took it. While he held it, he asked, "Now, about that other piece you were wanting?"

"Oh, I still want it. Trust me on that." I moved on to the carved lamp base that featured a buck and a doe."

Turning to Faye, I asked, "Don't you think Mel will just love it?"

Before she could answer, Dale asked, "This is for Mel? It's right up her alley, I guarantee it."

"Actually, it's for the guest room in her house. It will go well with a carved bedroom suite I found for in there."

"Oh, well don't be surprised if she wants it in her den when she sees it, is all I'm saying."

We talked lamp shades while Dale picked up the base and moved it to his register and I followed. He rang me up for that but held me off on paying for the dry sink.

"Now, now," he said, "Faye here knows I don't take payment for nothin' until it's in your hands. You just give me a good number to reach you at and I'll get back to you, probably Friday, when that sinks stained and it's had time to dry."

"Fair enough."

He began rummaging in a stack of boxes behind him, I presumed, for a box to put my new prize in. Faye idly mentioned, "It's so sad about Terry, don't you think?"

Turning away from his task, eyes narrowed, he replied, "Says you!"

I was taken aback by the venom in his tone but Faye didn't seem nearly as fazed. "What's got you all wrapped around the axel?" she asked him.

"Really, I shouldn't say anything now that he's gone and all but that guy just always rubbed me the wrong way. Terry was a cheat at cards, at fishing, at hunting…whatever he could cheat at."

Faye just nodded at the man, encouraging him while giving me an 'I told you so' look.

Dale kept right on going, "He pissed me off bad a few years back. Me and a buddy were out hunting. I shot an 11 point buck I'd been scouting for weeks. I hit it good but it still had the gumption to take off. By the time I got out of my stand, followed the blood trail and chased it down, Terry had found it and claimed it as one he'd shot and he and a buddy of his were already field dressing it." Dale shook with rage as he recalled the events.

"Then," he continued, "to add insult to injury, Terry had the rack mounted and he hung it on the wall in his den at home. Every time I was there after that it was as though the buck was staring down at me, taunting me while we played cards whenever we played there. And, to top it off, he always cheated when we were at his place too!"

I was curious, "Why on earth did you keep playing cards with him after that and after...well, knowing that he cheats?"

"You know, we had this group see, and Terry was always a part of it. Despite the cheating at everything, he was a likeable enough guy just to *talk to*. There just aren't too many guys my age around here anymore that would get together for things like poker." He shrugged, "You just had to watch him real close like, and not let him get away with any of his crap and boy did he like to pull some crap..."

"Let's stop at Sharpe's."
"I don't think there's anything else in her shop we'd want for the girls, Faye."

"Probably not; I think you cleaned her out of her good stuff yesterday but she's always good for tea and a little gossip."

Smiling at that, I thought to myself, Faye's trying to put her mind at rest about Terry.

I was right; as soon as Lucy Sharpe saw Faye, she greeted us both but then, turning directly to Faye, she started in on that very topic.

"I heard last night that Terry had passed on, God rest his soul."

"Yes…well, actually Lucy, he drowned in Chuck's pond."

The older woman clucked her tongue. "What a horrible way to go." She looked back to me, "Where are my manners? How did that bedroom set turn out in Melissa's guest room?"

"It looks lovely Mrs. Sharpe."

"Oh call me Lucy please. I'm glad you like it there dear. Now then, you're here about the same time as you were yesterday and right about the time I always take a little tea. Would you two join me?" Her look was expectant.

"Of course," Faye smiled.

We took seats while Lucy bustled about setting out tea in dainty, fussy little cups different from the ones she and I had used just the day before.

When she'd finally settled herself at the table, she picked right back up where she'd left off about Terry, "I hope," she said, "that he's less restless in death than he was in life."

This time I asked, "What makes you say that?"

Lucy glanced at Faye and then back to me, "Oh, you know; Terry…he was a bit of a philanderer."

Faye nodded knowingly.

Leaning forward conspiratorially, Lucy went on, "He once tried to hit on Rich Johnson's wife, Amy. She was having none of it but Rich was livid anyway, when he found out. He confronted Terry about it. They never had two kind words to say to each other after that. Terry was never one to take blame or to try and make amends."

We passed an easy half hour talking about this, that and everything else between us then I used Dana's bank card to buy them a nice wall clock for their still empty living room and we moved on.

When we were back in Jesse's pickup, I confronted Faye. "Who are Rich and Amy Johnson?"

"Rich is an oil field worker. He's only in his early forties, I'd say. His wife Amy is an attractive homemaker and I want to say she's in her late thirties but she looks even younger. They have two teenaged children though that she gave birth to so she's got to be well out of her twenties."

"Seems a little young for Terry."

"It doesn't surprise me," was all Faye said, seemingly wanting to close the subject.

"Where to next?"

"I thought I'd take you to see a couple of the local Amish craftsman and get a feel for what's out there. If you like their stuff but you want to see a bit more, tomorrow we can go up to Berlin and visit among the shops there; that's quite an experience in itself."

"Hmm, well, today sounds like a plan but tomorrow I think I really need to focus on finding some comfortable living room furniture for them. Their whole camping cot motif just isn't getting it for me." We both had a little laugh at that.

Faye pulled the loaded pickup up to the fuel pump. While she filled the tank, I went inside the station and availed myself of the ladies room. I just couldn't hold it for that last block and a half back to the girls house.

We'd spent a long going from place to place and we did pretty well, all told. There was the minor glitch of the Amish not taking Dana's card but, it all worked out once I called her and cajoled a pin out of her and took as much cash out of an ATM as it would let me have.

Just as I returned to the truck, an older woman approached us and greeted Faye with a bright smile.

Faye spotted as she hung up the pump nozzle, "Well hello there Jenna Mae; how in the world are you?"

Spotting me, she immediately introduced me to the much older woman, "Jenna Mae, this is Chloe Rossi, a new friend of mine. Chloe, this is Jenna Mae Rogers, one of the matriarchs of our little village here."

I took the woman's hand in both of mine. "I'm so pleased to meet you. This really is a lovely village, just a great place to live from what I've seen of it."

Jenna Mae beamed at first. "It really is lovely; thank you for saying so," but then her face grew troubled. She looked back at Faye as I released her hand, "Isn't it just terrible though, what's happened to poor Terry?"

"Yes," Faye replied. "May God rest his soul."

We all nodded solemnly.

"I just hate to think how he went out, is all. That's got to weigh heavily on Sheila's mind, after all."

"Yes, drowning is a horrible way to go. Just horrible." Faye shook her head while I stood by wordlessly.

"Well, that too, but I meant that they seemed to be having a lovers quarrel before he stormed off and all and went fishing in the first place."

Shocked yet again, I shot Faye a look. She shrugged her response in return.

"Mrs. Rogers," I began gently, "I was actually in the store picking up a few things when Terry left it Sunday morning. I admit, I don't really know them but nothing seemed terribly amiss."

"Oh dear, how shall I put this?" Jenna Mae looked truly uncomfortable. She was quiet for several long moments and then mumbled, "Perhaps I should just leave it lie."

Faye placed a hand on the older woman's arm and patted it. "It's okay. You can tell us and get it off your chest."

"I suppose you're right." She paused again but then she seemed to gather herself, "I was on my way up to church. I usually walk but I drove that day because Terry left a message on that machine thing I have that my canning lids were in. I knew he'd be in there, so I stopped for them. I didn't expect Sheila to be there but there she was and it was obvious they had been arguing before I even walked in. I could hear them"

"They quieted down quick enough though. I don't even know why Sheila was there at all. She's always at church on Sunday and she almost never works in the store on the Lords day. Terry, well, he stopped coming to church a couple of years ago." She looked at me, "You say you saw them later?"

I nodded. "Yes, and now that I think about it, Sheila

seemed a little annoyed at Terry but I wrote that off to having to go in there to help him rather than go to church."

"Maybe that's it then." She nodded to herself and then repeated a bit louder, "Maybe that's it."

As Faye and I toted our smaller purchases into Dana and Mel's home, we talked more about Terry.

"I admit," Faye said, "I was starting to think maybe Jesse was right. There do seem to be a few people out there that had it in for the man but, from what Jenna Mae said, an argument between him and Sheila could have happened and maybe he took having to go to the back for something for you as an excuse to just leave and go and cool off."

"You're probably right."

* * *

Thursday morning, October 16th, 2014

I slept well in the girls guest room which I thought was coming together quite nicely, in fact, almost too well. It was nearly 9:00 AM when I ventured downstairs.

Deciding I needed a good cuppa to really get me started for the day, I filled the coffee maker and flipped it on. I was distressed to find that the little creamer container I'd grabbed after the reception had less than a teaspoon left in it though. While the pot brewed, I slipped on my shoes, grabbed my keys and prayed the gas station had at least one overpriced container I could buy.

Surprised to see the open sign on at the store just half a block up the street, I pulled in there instead. Sheila herself and a young girl were sitting outside on a bench. I walked up to them tentatively.

"My condolences," I told her. "I'm so sorry if I'm mistaken; I didn't think you'd be open."

Sheila half smiled, "I forgot to cancel the usual deliveries. Since I had to be here for them anyway, I just opened up." She got up from the bench and led the way inside. The girl stayed put. "How can I help you?"

I told her what I needed and she pointed it out straight away. I was quiet as she rang up large container I'd chosen. As she started to thank me, a delivery driver came through the front door and addressed her so I just melted away.

Outside, the girl was still on the bench, kicking one foot back and forth. I guessed she must be about ten or twelve. Looking at her closely, I could see a family resemblance to Sheila.

"I'm really sorry to hear about your grandpa."

She tilted her head and peered up at me, "This was his favorite bench. He always told me he was just gonna' sit here all day and watch the world go by."

Skeptical about much of the world passing him on the only paved road in and out of Morelville, I nevertheless smiled and nodded at the obviously grieving youngster. A thought coming to mind, I asked her, "Your grandma got a little busy in there. You don't happen to know when the funeral is, do you?"

"Not till Saturday. That's when everyone can get here."

"Oh, I see. Well I'll certainly be there."

"Did you know him ma'am?"

"I'd only just met him but my daughter-in-law knows him well; Melissa Crane?"

"You're related to Sheriff Mel? She's so cool! I'm Emily, by the way. I'm 13. Sheriff Mel comes to our school and talks to us about things like bullies and drugs and stuff."

"That's great that she does that."

Emily nodded. "Will she be at the funeral too?"

"I don't know. She's away right now but she may come back in time for it."

"Oh." The girl seemed a little disappointed.

I changed the topic back to her grandpa, "Did you sit her with your grandpa a lot?"

"Papaw? No. Just sometimes in the summer when I'm not in school. Mostly he took me fishing. I saw him carrying his favorite pole and his creel that he only uses sometimes into the store the day that he…that he died. I was kind of upset when I found out he went fishing without me…we were supposed to go after he closed up for the day." She sniffled and then wailed, "If only I had been there." Tears started streaming down her face.

"Oh sweetie, what happened isn't your fault." I tried my best to comfort her while in my head I was thinking; *Why did he bring his fishing gear into the store and what happened to his creel? Wouldn't Sheila have noticed them being here if she had been in the back at all?*

Sheila, as my son Vince puts it, suddenly became a person of interest to me. In my mind, this was starting to become a curious case after all.

* * *

I was trying to arrange items attractively on a couple of book cases in the living room when a horn sounded in the driveway. When I stuck my head out the door, Faye yelled, "Come on! Grab a little cash. I'm taking you to the 'Bent 'n Dent."

"What in the world is a bent and dent?" I asked, as I climbed into Jesse's pickup yet again.

"An Amish run grocery that's just what the name implies. Everything is dirt cheap, just watch your dates."

Twenty minutes down a couple of old dirt roads later, we pulled into a gravel parking lot with plenty of room for cars and hitching posts for horse and buggy outfits. *Yet another adventure with Faye!*

Half an hour and fifty dollars later, I walked out of there with two Amish boys trailing me, each of us carrying a box load of stuff to fill Dana and Mel's cupboards. I was pretty pleased with myself and even happier that Faye had introduced me to this out of the way treasure of a place.

Faye placed her own single box of items in the bed of the truck and then hopped back in behind the wheel. "Girl; you did good!"

I smiled. "That was quite the experience."

"You're about to get another one; if you don't mind, that is?"

"Lead on. Where are we going?"

"Just over to the feed store. Jesse needs me to pick up something but they have kennels with lots of puppies to look at and play with usually…" Faye trailed off but raised her eyebrows at me and grinned.

I thought of my own little dog Lady, back at the house,

all alone. Back in McKeesport, she went wherever I went.

When we arrived, Faye pointed out the kennels and I headed straight back there while she went inside the busy looking feed mill to conduct her business. By the time she came out, I'd fallen head over heels for a cute little Boston terrier pup that was the runt of her mama's litter. She was weaned and ready to go. I just had to have her for Dana.

Faye walked in as the young Amish girl was writing up my bill of sale. She'd agreed to take my check so we were in business.

"Chloe, what are you doing with that dog?"

"I'm buying her. Isn't she precious?"

"Adorable, but you already have a dog."

"Well this one will keep Lady company while I'm here but she's not for me."

Faye raised an eyebrow, "Who, pray tell, is she for?"

"Dana, of course. Oh, I hope Mel won't mind but Dana loves dogs and this is just what she needs, an energetic little girl like this to get her up and moving on that leg of hers."

"Mel likes dogs too but she likes big dogs like labs... not...not little foo foo dogs."

"Faye! A Boston terrier is hardly foo foo! They're very playful dogs. Those two will have great fun with little Boo here."

"Boo?"

I nodded and grinned at the dog I was now cradling, "Boo."

CHAPTER 12

Positive ID

Thursday Afternoon, October 15th, 2014
Gatlinburg, Tennessee

I was grilling a couple of great looking steaks we'd bought at a market we stopped at in Sevierville on our way back to the cabin from a day at Douglas Lake when my cell rang. I checked the number before I bothered to answer it.

"Sorry babe. It's Izzy from the lab." Dana was standing at the table by the deck rail. She stopped breaking up lettuce for salad and nodded for me to go ahead and take it.

"Izzy?"

"Yeah Mel; it's me."

"I sure didn't expect to hear back from you so soon."

"Your prints came in on the early FedEx run this morning and it's been a slow business day here."

"Really? Slow?"

"No. I lied but I worked you in. You owe me Mel."

"Gotcha. Any hits?"

"Yeah; like I said, you owe me."

"I know it and you know I'm good for it. What did you find?"

"What are you really doing down there in Tennessee?"

"You know I'm on my honeymoon. Why? What does

that have to do with anything?"

"You didn't head down there on purpose to work a case, honestly?"

"No; I didn't." I was suspicious now, "Tell me what you found."

"Mel, the prints came back as belonging to a Terry Ford, last known address, *Morelville, Ohio*. He's in AFIS due to a DUI arrest way back in February of 2003."

Dana was incredulous, "What are the odds?"

"Slow down babe; way, way down. Look, I got the cabin company recommendation for down here *from Terry*. I told you that. You know this area but I didn't and he's originally from around here. He has family, including his brother Pete, still in the area somewhere near here."

I took a deep breath and gathered my thoughts. "I wasn't sure exactly where but I knew Terry would come down here to hunt and sometimes, when family stuff was going on, he said he would even bring Sheila down if she wanted to come. It's plausible that he or both of them may have stayed in this cabin at some point in the very recent past. I'd have to look at that a lot closer."

"Let's look at it logically: what would Terry have come down here to hunt for in September? We've already checked, nothing was technically in season. Don't you think if he was coming to hunt he would have just waited until bow season opened in October or gun season in November? Is he the type that would he risk taking game out of season or is he the type that would have come here just for the coyote hunt?"

"I don't know. I can't answer any of that. On the flip side, maybe him being here wasn't about hunting at all. Maybe Sheila was here and they were having a little get-away before Patricia came along and rented this cabin too."

"You know, I don't buy it. It's very odd that an Ohio woman died here; a woman that, may I remind you we know was often seen around here with a man and that Terry's prints are here – very near to the Jacuzzi tub where the woman died – and now, on top of it all, Terry's dead back in Morelville."

"It could all be a very strange coincidence." I shrugged. Without access to anything that had been found back in Morelville, I was at a total loss.

"Do you think it's a coincidence *Sheriff Crane*?"

She has me there. I sighed, "No; I have to admit, it seems pretty fishy. Where would we even begin though? The local yokels are no help. Sad to say, but I don't trust Sheriff Trainor as far as I can throw him. And now, given Terry's death, all signs would seem to point toward Sheila Ford. That said, for the record, Sheila's a good woman. I can't picture her doing anything untoward. There has to be an explanation for Terry's prints being here that doesn't involve anything more sinister than maybe an extramarital affair and his death now is probably just a freak accident."

"Mel, think about what you just said."

I spread my hands, "What…what did I say?"

"If Terry was here, having an affair with Patricia, he may have killed her, staged the scene and then left before Trainor and crew got here. Hell, maybe he was in some sort of cahoots with Trainor and that's why their 'so called' investigation was so botched."

"Any way we slice it, what a mess…"

CHAPTER 13

The Sordid Side

Mama Rossi
Thursday Evening, October 15th, 2014
Morelville

Faye and I were sitting at the table in Mel and Dana's newly decorated kitchen having a little coffee and conversation about the things I'd done to the house.

"You haven't gotten into Zanesville or Columbus yet for living room furniture though, I noticed."

"No; there just hasn't been time. Maybe tomorrow…do you want to go?" I looked at Faye hopefully.

"Sorry but I'm all booked up. Jesse has errands for me to run for him in the morning and then the varsity plays tomorrow night. Cole has to be there even though he's just on the JV team right now. I'll be running around like a mad woman trying to get everything done in time to corral him and Beth from school, get them fed and then get him back there."

"That's okay. I probably should let them have one room to decorate themselves, anyway. Do you need some help tomorrow with all of the stuff on your list?"

Before she could answer me, her daughter Kris's kids Beth and Cole struggled through the door from the driveway between this house and their own home just across from it. Boo yipped at them and attacked their ankles as they tried to maneuver with the piles of hoodies and jackets Faye had run them into town to get. She was getting an able assist from my five year old dog Lady. Boo had brought a sense of playfulness out of Lady in just a few hours with her that I thought was gone.

We laughed over the dogs for a few more minutes and chatted a bit more then Faye drained her cup and got up to rinse it. "We best get going. They have school in the morning and, like I said, I've got a million things to do. I have to remember to make something for Terry's wake too, now that I think about it."

"I, uh, met his granddaughter Emily this morning. She told me the funeral is Saturday."

Faye shook her head, "Yes, the viewing is tomorrow evening and then the funeral is at 2:00 on Saturday. I suppose I should call Mel and let her know. She may want to come back tomorrow and…"

Beth interrupted her grandmother by addressing me, "You met Emily?"

"Yes, today. She was sitting on the bench outside of her Papaw's store."

"I wish I had seen her. She's pretty messed up about the whole thing. I called her because she hasn't been at school all week."

"Emily and Beth are very close; they're in the same grade," Faye supplied.

"I see." Smiling softly at Beth, I told her, "It's normal for children to grieve when they lose loved ones." I knew from

Dana that Beth and Cole had recently lost their father. I was trying to be gentle in my response.

"It's not that. Emily's other grandpa, Grandpa Art, and her Papaw Terry used to be best of friends. Now her other grandpa is saying he won't even go to the funeral."

"Really," Faye asked, "Why is that?"

"They were fighting over something stupid like you're always telling me 'n Cole not to fight over…some fancy fishing reel or something. Emily said her Papaw Ford bought it cheap at some yard sale and said he would sell it to her Grandpa Majors but then he didn't. Emily said it was a Garcia something or other and it was actually worth a lot of money. Mr. Majors called Mr. Ford an old conniver and said he wasn't going to his funeral."

"He'll probably change his mind sweetie," Faye told Beth. "He's just angry right now."

"Emily told me that happened months ago and they haven't spoken since, so I don't know. I don't think he will."

I questioned Faye, "Did Terry use the reel?"

"Not that I'm aware of but I wouldn't know anyway. I don't fish. Jesse would know better than I." She paused, seeming to be thinking, "Knowing Terry, he probably sold it for more money than Art was going to give him for it or maybe he just put it away for another time."

"Maybe he taunted Art with it?"

"Not if they weren't speaking like Emily told Beth, which, with those two, was pretty likely. They would have avoided each other…the two stubborn old fools."

"You know what? That reminds me of something else Emily told *me* today." I told Faye about Terry having his rod and his creel basket with him at the store on Sunday. "Sheila probably saw it Faye because Emily sure did. She had to suspect Terry was going fishing at some point that day so why didn't she say anything about that when he disappeared and she reported him missing?"

Faye shifted her eyes to Beth and Cole waiting by the door, soaking in every word and then she shifted them back to me. I shut up and let my mind run.

Pointing at the pile of clothes and coats the kids had dumped in a chair I had temporarily sitting where the dry sink was going to go, she said, "Take those to the truck. I'll be out in a minute." She handed Cole the keys.

She watched them until they were both in the truck and out of earshot and then she said, "Chloe, Terry was married before. He's only been with Sheila for about 10 years and he hasn't always been faithful to her, to hear it told. What we heard from Lucy Sharp yesterday about him hitting on Amy was news to me but it wasn't a real surprise either and Jenna Mae telling us she heard them arguing supports that. He probably did something to tick Sheila off and, when he left, she just blocked everything else out."

She continued, "True or not, Sheila has still had other ups and downs with him but, through it all, she's stuck by him. I give her a lot of credit for that." With that, Faye said goodbye, told me she'd call me in the morning, and took her leave.

Her statements cemented Sheila as a suspect in my mind but, in deference to Faye, who was obviously fond of the woman, I kept those thoughts to myself.

CHAPTER 14

On the Road

Mel
Friday, October 16th, 2014
Gatlinburg, Tennessee

I cut a bite out of the stack of pancakes with fruit topping and popped it in my mouth. The zing of the cherries sent a shiver down my spine. Dana watched me, amusement lighting her eyes.

"Usually I'm the one clamoring for the next meal. It's funny to watch you get so into your food."

"These are amazing. You should try them."

"No thanks. I felt like having an omelet today."

"Omelet at a pancake house, that's…that's," I searched for the word, "blasphemy! That's what that is." We both laughed. "Seriously though, I'm really going to miss this… all of this. Just you and me, the mountains, doing what we want, eating what we want…no work…"

"Mel, you have more than a hundred grand socked away and, with my settlement I have a million plus and a lifetime pension. We don't *ever* have to go back to work if we don't want to."

I chuckled and then reminded her, "You *had* a million plus. You let your mother have free rein with your bank card, remember?"

Dana rolled her eyes. "I know but she promised to stick to working on the house and, I'll deny I ever said this, but I trust her. She'll do right by us."

"Oh, I don't doubt it for a minute."

"Back to my original statement; work? No work?"

"Baby, I love what I do and I just stood for election. I have a chance to make some real changes to the way policing is handled in Muskingum County. I at least want to see one term through."

"Okay, fair enough."

"Is it though?"

"Is it what?"

"Fair? I want to be fair to you too, to us as a couple too."

"I'll be honest; I've thought a lot about what I want to do next over the past couple of months and, believe it or not, even this week, down here, away from everything else. And, well, I don't think I want to go back into law enforcement or security. In fact, I know I don't."

"What do you want to do?"

"First off, I'd like to do more of this…just getting away, relaxing, recharging. I was thinking maybe we could look into buying a little place near a lake in Ohio or even…even a cabin down here in the mountains or along Douglas Lake that we could maybe get away to once in a while."

I grinned. "Baby, I'm all for either one of those. I love it down here and my immediate gut feeling is to get a place around here but, on the other hand, I also have to consider how much we can be here given the distance. We might make it down for a few long weekends a year these next four years, if we're lucky. Maybe somewhere in Ohio would be better…not so far so we could get there more often, huh?"

"Mel, I'd be okay with a few times a year for just a couple of days or we could even fly into Knoxville once in a while, cut the trip down to just a couple of hours of flying and driving. We'll figure it out. There's time for that. I have our first house to finish first."

"Yeah, but something tells me your mom isn't leaving you a lot to do. Either way, setting up housekeeping in a couple of places isn't going to keep you busy forever. What else did you have in mind?"

Dana's eyes shone. "I'd like to write a little…I've always wanted to do that. I have a lot of ideas for stories; I've been jotting them down for weeks and…well, beyond that, I don't know."

"Write, as in writing books and stuff?" She nodded. "I had no idea you wanted to do that but I think it's great." I smiled as my mind whirled, "We could set you up a nice little writer's retreat out on the back of the lot where you could be away from all the hubbub of my crazy family and just write your little heart out."

"Or, since I'm only talking about a *part time* writing venture here, we could share the office we already have in the house that you'll hardly ever use…"

"True," I told her, "but my piebald mount stays."

"Deal!"

I smiled. "I love you Dana."

"I love you too."

My phone buzzed in my pocket as we were combing

through the little gift shop in the restaurant after breakfast. I glanced at the text from Beth and then showed it to Dana:

Beth: Grandma said to let you know that Terry's funeral is Saturday at 2:00.

Me: Okay. Thanks kiddo. Now put your phone away before you get caught!

I grinned at Dana, "They're not supposed to use them in school except at lunch time."

"Do you want to head back today so we can go to the funeral?"

"I don't want to short change our honeymoon Dana. Who knows when we'll get to get away again? It may be a while."

"It's okay; really. We can come down here again, just like we talked about. Right now, you should be there and I'm on pins and needles to see what my mother's been up to myself. And, if we go back, you can kind of get a little jump on Monday too so you're not so stressed."

"I do sort of want to poke around the whole Patricia Dunkirk/Terry Ford thing and see if there's anything to it – anything at all between them – and I need to follow up on the Harper investigation. My guys insisted they wouldn't call me on my honeymoon and they haven't so I don't have a clue what's going on with that. It *would* be *real nice* not to be blindsided by everything on Monday."

"There you go then. Let's go get packed up."

CHAPTER 15

Manicures and Truth

Mama Rossi
Friday Morning, October 16th, 2014
Morelville

I had an inkling the girls would be home early so they could go to Terry's funeral. I figured I better get myself to the market and pick up a few perishables to stock their fridge.

All prepared to drive into Zanesville, I noticed the 'open' sign was on again in the village general store so I stopped there instead. I admit I was more than a little curious.

Sheila's employee was standing at the register but Sheila herself was slicing deli meat for a lone customer. I gathered milk and juice and a few other things up from the coolers and carried them to the counter and then waited while the other woman rang the customer out and Sheila washed up.

The girl behind the registered greeted me cordially and I smiled back but my eyes were on Sheila as she turned from the little sink behind the long counter and inspected her nails. Shaking her head, she looked up to find my eyes on her.

"I'm so sorry for staring," I said. "I really didn't expect to see you here today at all."

"We're going into the weekend so we really needed to be

open…what with expenses and all. Besides, the phone has done nothing but ring. I just had to get out of the house and away from it today." She looked over my purchases as the other woman bagged them.

"Well, again, my condolences. I don't know that Melissa and Dana will make it back in time for calling hours tonight but we're assuming they'll be in late or early in the morning so I bought a few provisions for them."

Sheila half smiled as she gripped the counter edge.

I reached over and picked up her hand in mine, "Pardon my forwardness, but I saw you inspecting these a minute ago." I ran a thumb along her nails. "I'm a nail tech and I'd be happy to do these for you before the viewing this evening…if you like."

"Would you? Oh, that would be wonderful. I'd pay you of course."

"Oh no, I couldn't possibly accept payment at a time like this. I'd do it for anyone."

Sheila thought a minute then nodded, "Okay then."

"Where and when would you like me to do them? I have everything I need here with me because I always take it everywhere with me but, since Mel and Dana are just moving into their new home, there really isn't a suitable place there to do it yet."

"There isn't any place we can do it here either." She looked at her helper who promptly volunteered to man the store if Sheila wanted to head home.

I agreed to meet her there after I put my purchases away and gathered my kit and she gave me simple directions to get there.

Viva Mama Rossi!

Ten minutes later, food put away and nail care kit assembled, I arrived at the Ford home and tapped lightly on Sheila's front door. When she let me in, I immediately apologized for having to have her come back to her own home. "I know you were trying to get away from the phone for a bit, dear."

"It's okay. There was just as much hubbub in the store. At least here I can just let voicemail pick up the calls." She pointed to a digital set on the corner of the kitchen counter as we took seats in her windowed breakfast nook.

"I'm surprised you have a landline phone at all."

"Oh, you have to way out here. Cell phone service is so spotty no matter what those darn companies say otherwise. We…I get it through the cable company so it's not too bad. Other people who can't get cable out to their places pay a fortune to have a home phone."

We took seats but she jumped back up, "I'm so sorry. Can I get you some coffee or some tea, maybe?"

"That's kind but no thank you. I try not to have anything spill-able nearby while I'm working because I'll surely spill it."

Sheila grinned, "This is kind *of you*."

I smiled back at her and asked her what she'd like done then I began to work, mostly in silence as she just watched what I was doing but, gradually, she began to relax and ask questions. We began to talk about this and that after that, making light conversation.

She started to tell me something about one of her grandchildren when the sound of the phone ringing interrupted her.

"Did you want to answer that?"

"Let me just listen first and see who it is."

I nodded and continued about my task. After four or five rings, her machine picked up and a woman's voice came over the little speaker;

"Hi Sheila, it's Pam Walter's…I, uh just wanted to offer my condolences on your loss. I know it must be hard. I'm going to try to come to the viewing but, well…I don't know about Dale…you know… Anyway, I'm really sorry…" We could both hear the sound of a door opening and a man's voice calling out, "Pam!" "Oops," Pam continued, "Dale's home for lunch; gotta' run. Bye!"

I didn't say anything to Sheila about her caller but I guessed that I must have just heard the voice of the wife of Dingy Dale who didn't completely share her husband's mostly negative view of the deceased Terry Ford.

As I was cleaning up about a half hour after that call came through and a couple more less interesting ones, Sheila inspected my handiwork and offered to pay me again.

"Nonsense," I told her. "You don't owe me a thing."

She shook her head, "These look great. Can I ask, what do you normally charge for what you've done for me?"

"Well, you've just gotten the basic manicure, a simple repair and a polish job. Your nails were in pretty good shape. Back in Pittsburgh, where I'm from, I'd have charged you $30 for that. For a full set of nails it would have been more and for appliques more again. The works would have been pretty expensive at $65-75."

Sheila didn't wince. Instead, she said, "Oh honey, that's what they charge at the only nail salon in Zanesville too for everything! Just a manicure and polish though will cost you $45.00 there. It's just crazy…looking good is soooo expensive! I'll tell you this, lots of women around here would love to have another option and, if it's a slightly less expensive one…" She nudged me gently with an elbow, protecting her still tacky wet polish job.

"It's certainly a thought. I contract out of a shop for some things and work on my own for some established clients. I buy all my own supplies either way, but for the shop work, I have to kick back a sitting fee."

"Maybe you ought to consider making a change." Sheila half shrugged.

"A change would be nice but, on the other hand, I do have a husband and a home back there to get back to."

Oddly, I thought, Sheila's look didn't grow wistful or darken as I suspected it might after I mentioned my own husband. Instead, she suggested I give some thought to visiting Morelville more often.

She thanked me as she showed me to a side door just off the nook area where we'd spent our time. I took note of a .22 single shot rifle sitting in the corner by the door like the one my Mario uses all the time for rabbit hunting.

I tipped my head at the gun, "Does everyone around here keep a gun so handy?"

"Oh, that's Terry's…was Terry's. He didn't like having a shotgun near the door like most people out here seem to do. Too dangerous…we've had problems with groundhogs.

The .22 was good for that." Her eyes never met mine as she spilled out her little speech.

* * *

It wasn't hard for me to find the little funeral parlor where Terry's viewing was being held. There only seemed to be one in Morelville and there was a line out the door of people waiting to pay their respects, if not Terry specifically, at least to his widow and his family.

I fell into line behind a gentleman who seemed to be waiting alone. Ahead, I could see Faye and Jesse Crane. I did my best to keep several mourners between myself and Faye's line of sight.

A gentleman stepped up to the line and fell in behind me. The man in front of me greeted him quietly and they began to converse with each other around me. The first man politely insisted I take his place and he stepped back to stand next to the second man while they waited.

Ahead of me, almost to the Cranes, most people were alone and seemed to have come directly from work, judging by their attire. It was a somber line with little chatter going on. I'd resigned myself to a fruitless wait when the hushed conversation behind me grew far more interesting than it had been.

The gentleman who arrived after me asked the first fellow, "Has Art Majors been through already or do you know if he's coming?"

"No idea," the first man there replied. "I do know they hadn't been speaking at all before Terry died; it's such a shame."

"They always were like oil and water, those two," man two said.

"This time it's silly though. They were squabbling over some fancy Abu Garcia fishing reel, of all things, and Art claims it was the last straw. Said he didn't want anything more to do with Terry. Stupid…"

Man two spoke again, "I agree but I think there's more to it than just that."

"I hear he actually told Chuck he isn't sorry the man is dead. Can you believe he actually said that about someone who's passed on? Terry Ford was no saint, I admit, but dishonoring the dead because you're bitter about not getting something for a steal is just so uncharitable." His voice had risen a little but he quieted down when his friend repeated, "Bud, I think there's more to it."

"How so? Do you know something I don't?"

Did you hear about the camper…well, I guess we should call it an RV, deal?"

"RV Deal?"

The second man must have nodded because the first, after a beat, said, "No."

"Art's grandson has a buy here/pay here used car lot just outside of Zanesville. He let some guy trade a high end, decked out RV for an F-250 that someone else with more money than sense traded there. The kid couldn't move the RV because no one visiting his lot could afford what it was worth. Art tried to help him out; gave him a loan to get it fully inspected, get it detailed and to advertise it around outside the local area. He sunk a few grand in which he would have gotten back with a little interest when it sold. The advertising was all paid for and running and along comes Terry…says he wants it."

"Let me guess, he wanted a deal?"

"Right," guy two says. "He gets the kid to sell it to him for a grand above what the truck trade was worth just to, he says, 'get it out of his hair.' Thing is, it was worth at least twenty grand more than that truck. The kid makes next to nothing and Art's out a few grand. Art was livid and he let Terry have it but the kid made the deal. Terry didn't force him to take it."

"So where's the RV now?"

"Terry turned around and sold it for, I hear, ten grand more than he paid and didn't give Art a dime of it."

CHAPTER 16

Home Sweet Home?

Mel
Friday Evening, October 16th, 2014
Morelville

We'd gotten packed up and checked out of our cabin by 11:00. There was no refund for the missed night. I didn't figure there would be. It would have been nice to stay on and enjoy a final afternoon and evening of rest and relaxation, especially since it was paid for, but I knew my duty was back at home.

Once we were on the road, we meandered back to Ohio, taking our time. Neither of us was actually ready to call an end to the honeymoon just yet. When we finally drove into the village, it was nearly 10:00 PM. Chloe's car was in the driveway next to my truck but the house appeared dark and quiet.

I unloaded our bags while Dana stretched out her legs, both…not just the injured one. She moved toward the door before I was finished. Coming up the side porch steps behind her, I watched her insert her key into the lock but then pause and listen intently.

She turned to me, "Do you hear that?"

"Sounds like a dog somewhere in there…"

"Not *a* dog…*dogs*. I know mama has Little Lady here but…" Dana pushed the door open and flipped on the overhead light then stopped dead in her tracks.

Our kitchen, formerly devoid of curtains, decorations and in need of a good scrubbing, was now decorated in fall colors and gleamed in every respect. A new microwave stood on the counter by the coffee maker Chloe had bought us as a wedding gift. No dogs or evidence of their existence was anywhere in sight though.

I cocked an ear and listened. I could hear one dog mewling from somewhere upstairs but only one. *Must have been our imaginations before…*

Dana wandered through the downstairs as I finished bringing our bags in. Returning to me, she shook her head, "It's a completely different house…completely."

I looked around myself. Our bedroom, already set up before we left, was untouched but, other than that, Chloe had cleaned and decorated the place like a mad woman. The kitchen still needed a dining table and the living room was devoid of most lounging furniture but a very nice entertainment center and a set of bookcases stood at the ready and partially full. There was even a little art on the freshly scrubbed walls.

"Your mom's amazing, babe!"

"You like it?"

"Yeah…yeah, I do. I'm not real crazy about the whole chicken motif in the kitchen but it still looks nice. What do you think?"

"I like it too. Here's the thing though…this probably isn't all."

I tipped my head and looked at my wife, "What do you mean?"

There's no sofa in here yet and the cot's gone. She's not sleeping in our room so she must have set up the guest room upstairs too."

"I'll bet you're right. Would she be asleep yet? Do you think she'd mind if we went and had a look?"

"With her dog yapping like that, she's probably awake and up there dying to know what we're thinking. I'm surprised she hasn't come down already. We should just go to bed and let her stew."

"That's just mean Dana, after all her hard work. Besides, *I'm* dying to see upstairs."

We mounted the steps and started up. By the time we hit the landing, it was very obvious there were two dogs behind a closed door in one of the upstairs rooms. One was whining and the other yapping. As we reached the second floor, the guestroom door swung inward revealing Dana's pajama clad mother with two balls of energy circling her feet.

A black and white terrier pup jolted past me and hurled itself at Dana. She bent and caught it on the fly. "Aren't you the cutest thing?" she asked the pup as she held its face close to her own. Looking at the pup and then at her mother, she asked, "Mama, where did she come from?"

"You like her?" Chloe asked.

"She's adorable. Does dad know you got another dog?"

"Um…not exactly."

"Mama!"

"It's not mine Dana, baby."

"*Whose is it* Mama?" Dana's tone was suspicious.

"I picked her out for you."

"For me?" Dana asked while, at the same time I asked, "For her?" as I pointed at Dana.

We were still standing in the middle of the hallway. Dana put the pup down and it started circling between her and me."

"You two said you wanted a dog. She's a cutie and she'll be so good for you Dana. She's got plenty of energy but she won't pull you along on walks, and…"

"But a Boston Terrier?" I was in shock. "Chloe, I really appreciate what you were trying to do, but…"

"But what? You don't like little Boo, do you?"

"Boo?" we both asked, in unison.

"That's what I've been calling her. I got her just yesterday but she already seems to be adjusting to it…oops, looks like she might need to go outside. I better run her out." Chloe scooped up the dog and was down the steps with Little Lady trailing them leaving us both standing there slack jawed at her sudden exit, mid confrontation.

When the kitchen door banged, I turned to face Dana and asked, "So, you like the dog?"

"She is cute, babe. I take it you don't like her?"

"It's not that. It's just that I wanted, you know, a *real* dog."

"Pardon?"

"A real dog…a hunting dog or a working dog. Something bigger and not…prissy."

"Oh. Okay then…"

Dana's look was crestfallen. *She's fallen for the dog already. Now what do I do?* I thought fast, "Maybe we get two dogs?"

"That would be okay with you?" She looked at me hopefully.

I nodded and pulled her in for a quick kiss. Loosening my grip on her slim shoulders, I said, "We should probably head downstairs and meet her properly." I stepped back toward the stairs but Dana's touch stopped me.

"Let's look in there first," she pointed into the guest room where the glow of a bedside lamp was very apparent in a room that had neither a bedside table, a lamp or even a bed just a few days earlier.

We squeezed through the doorway together and were stopped short by the beauty of a carved, burled wood bed and matching dressing pieces. The carved lamp on the nightstand immediately caught my eye and drew me closer. Dana, meanwhile stood, fingers to her chin, and marveled at the bed.

"Mel, if this was a king size, I'd have you moving it downstairs this instant. It's gorgeous."

"Agreed."

She stared at me, "What are you doing?"

"This lamp is going across the hall, in the office." I had it unplugged and I was about to lift it off the stand.

"Seriously babe? It goes great in here. Just ask her where she got it and we'll get you a matching one."

I made a pouty face which got me a gentle backhand to the shoulder.

"Let's go meet Boo."

"Okay," I said, "but we're not calling her that."

CHAPTER 17

Report!

Mel
0600 Saturday Morning, October 17th, 2014

I didn't tell my assistant Holly that I'd be in the office on Saturday. I knew she'd show up at some point during the day just to make sure everything was just so, figuring I'd pop in on Sunday. Holly was a sergeant in her own right and a longtime friend I'd come up through the ranks with. She was the ideal choice to be my right hand when I took over as Sheriff. If I could get in and out before she got here, it would be a coup that I could egg her about for days.

I looked at the electronic schedule she kept. Shane Harding, my lead investigator, was due in at 7:00. I left him a message to come up and see me once he got settled then I dived into nearly a weeks' worth of email.

Coming up for air about 6:30, I switched gears. When Shane got in, I wanted to talk about the Olivia Steirs murder and what role, if any, Nevil Harper Sr. had played in it and about Terry Ford. I went over to records, pulled the slim Ford file myself since no one was in yet, and skimmed it quickly. There were several statements but I was the most interested in Sheila Fords.

I read through her statement to the deputy that had

taken her missing persons report and then through the later statement after Terry had been found. Both were consistent in content. Nothing seemed amiss.

Leafing through the rest of the file, I noted brief statements by Chloe Rossi about Terry's disappearance and by my father about finding him. *When on earth did Chloe have time to make a sworn statement?*

Shane popped his head around my door frame about 7:10. "Welcome back boss!"

"I'd like to say it's good to be back but, really, I was enjoying the break."

"I bet. I haven't been down that way in a few years but I know it's beautiful this time of year."

"That it is. We hope to get down there more in the future. For now though, duty calls."

Shane smiled, "I'm assuming you want a run-down of all the open stuff?"

"Not everything…not today anyway. For now, just give me the highlights on the Steirs case and then let's talk about the Ford drowning."

Shane flipped open his notes, "We don't have a lot to go on, on the Steirs murder. There are no camera's with video footage of her front or back door or anywhere out in front of her condo. The back gate was locked as was the back door the day she was found but, if you remember right, we went right in the front door when we received the call. It was unlocked and slightly ajar. The perp may have gone in and out that way."

I nodded as he continued, "There are still no witnesses

that saw anything at all going on that day besides Nevil Harper Jr. now…nobody's come forward. Junior claims his father left the door ajar and he did too, when he left after phoning the murder in. He's back at work at the shop he was at before. I check up on him daily. We've taken his fingerprints. They're not in AFIS. We don't know yet if they're a match for the few we got when we dusted in the house but I imagine they'll match to the phone, at a minimum."

"What about his father?"

"That's the toughie. We tried to pull him in here Wednesday to get a statement. He wouldn't talk much; lawyered right up."

"That's interesting there," I was surprised. "Prints?"

"We didn't get them but we didn't need to. He's been arrested before so his prints are already in the system. The lab is a little slow, no response yet on match or no match for any of the prints from the scene to father or son." I made a mental note to call my buddy Izzy on Monday, even if it meant adding to the debt I already owed her.

"Unfortunately, that's all we've got boss."

"Let's hope the prints give us something, then."

Shane nodded. "Ford is pretty straightforward Sheriff. Kreskie ruled Ford's death a drowning with no evidence of any trauma. He's pegged the time of death at approximately 1:30 in the afternoon on Sunday. There were no signs of foul play in the area of the pond where he drowned; in fact, there were no signs of other humans being on the scene at all until the search team, which included your own father, got there."

"I read dad's statement. I also read Sheila Ford's and my wife's mother's statements."

"Ford's brother and, uh, your father were raising such a stink boss, we got all of those because we were trying to be real thorough."

Nodding myself, I said, "I appreciate that. The Coroner says the time of death was about 1:30? Sheila Ford would have still been at the store, I imagine."

"She was. We checked that."

"She couldn't have, say, *pushed* him in? Or, held him under, maybe?"

"No. She was at the store until after 3:00 with several witnesses who have verified that."

"Did anyone report any sort of argument between the two of them?"

"No. She admitted to me that she was disgruntled having to be in the store on a Sunday but she was quick to tell us that wasn't Terry's fault. A woman that works with Terry on Sunday called off at the last minute and the worker corroborates that."

"Okay. Sounds like you covered all the bases." I thought for a minute. "You know, what I don't understand is how a man drowns in such a shallow pond. I'm familiar with that one. We used to fish there with dad. It's a good sized one but, even out in the very center, it's maybe six feet deep."

"Boss, we both know you can drown in a lot less water than that. Maybe he fell in, got stuck in the muck and, fighting to get out, he took in too much water or got too far out where he panicked."

"Panicked? Why?"

"You don't know?"

"Know what?"

Shane's eyes bored into mine, "Ford couldn't swim Mel."
"Seriously?"
"Chuck Knox, the guy that owns the pond swore to that but, ask Terry's brother or any of his other fishing buddies Sheriff or look at any fishing derby pictures of him; he always has a lightweight life vest on. It was with his gear that was stacked at home by the front door ready for the fishing trip he was supposed to leave for on Monday morning. He went out that day without it."
"Well I'll be damned…"

I scribbled out a quick note for Holly from a rhyme I remembered from high school;

*I was here but now I'm gone,
I left this note to carry on…*

I put a bottle of Bennett's barbecue sauce, a gift for her, at the corner to hold it down. *That will get her all stirred up!*

To satisfy my own curiosity, I ran Joe Treadway down in town as he was leaving a radio call.
"Hey Sheriff. Welcome back."
"Thanks Joe. Got a minute?" He nodded. "I just talked with Harding but I want to get the scoop from someone that was on the scene at the Ford drowning when he was pulled out. What can you tell me?"
"There's not much to tell. From the set up, it looked like he was fishing from the bank, fell in for some reason or waded out and he drowned. There was no sign at all of any struggle and there was no sign of any other vehicle having

been in the area."

"Was he wearing waders Joe or muckin' boots, at least?"

"No," he shook his head. "Just regular ankle boots… hiking type boots."

"Was there any tackle or any bait around that might have been his?"

"That was the only odd thing Sheriff. His pole was there, line out in the water, but nothin' else. We did look around for stuff but we didn't find anything."

I nodded. "Okay then. That's odd but it's the only odd thing. It settles it in my mind."

"That all Sheriff?"

"One more thing Joe; will you be sitting for the detective test this time around? I still have a vacancy that needs filled. You'd do a fine job."

"No Sheriff; sorry to disappoint you but I like what I'm doin' just fine, if you don't mind. Somebody has to show these new patrol deputies how to do things right."

CHAPTER 18

Bereaved?

Mamma Rossi
Saturday Afternoon, October 17th, 2014

Dana and I walked into the church where Terry's memorial service was being held. It was only slightly larger than the funeral parlor just up the street where the viewing had been and it was filling up fast. We found seats together near the back with a little space left over for Mel when she arrived from work.

I knew from what I'd heard that Terry wasn't a churchgoer but his wife was. I watched as mourner after mourner approached her and offered condolences. Other people were present around her, presumably his children and grandchildren. Some were crying or looked near tears. The widow herself was somber in her black attire and muted expression but otherwise dry eyed.

I whispered to Dana, "It's not my place to judge but really, through this whole thing, she hasn't seemed too awfully upset." I tipped my head toward the standing Sheila Ford. My darling daughter didn't reply. She just shook her head slightly and continued to watch the goings on in front of the casket set front and center.

Mel, still in full uniform, joined us a few minutes before

the service began. Several rows ahead, on the other side of the only aisle, were the Cranes. They'd arrived, apparently, much earlier than we had. I didn't see Dingy Dale anywhere in the little church and I had no idea what the Johnsons or Art Majors looked like to know if any of them had decided to show up and pay their respects.

We three sat through a short, generic sermon by a pastor who obviously didn't know much about Terry and some more heart felt short eulogies from the man's grandchildren. A half hour later it was all over but the burial.

A caravan of cars proceeded out to the village cemetery. Dana and I left her car back at the church and rode with Mel. The two of them seemed preoccupied through the entire graveside thing. I noticed Mel watching Sheila a lot but I didn't know what to make of it.

Back at the church for the wake, we joined Faye and Jesse. Standing next to each other, serving food were none other than Lucy Sharpe and Jenna Mae Rogers. I was surprised but Faye seemed unfazed, greeting both women warmly.

"Chloe, you know Lucy and I introduced you to Jenna Mae the other day."

"I remember. It's such a somber occasion but it's nice to see you two ladies again." Both just nodded, Lucy Sharp's mouth set in a grim line and Jenna Mae smiling only slightly. I was a little put out by their demeanor but I tried not to let it show. Instead, I said, "Lucy, they just love that bedroom suite in the guest room!"

Lucy Sharpe turned to Mel, "Did you?"

Viva Mama Rossi!

"It's beautiful Mrs. Sharpe."

For my daughter-in-law she smiled brightly. "I'm so glad you like it dear."

We all continued past as the two women served the next people in line with bright smiles. *Well that's a puzzle, there!*

We all took seats at one end of long tables set up in the fellowship hall downstairs from the church sanctuary. The tables filled up as fast as the memorial service had.

I was sitting directly across from Faye. While Jesse was speaking over his shoulder to a man I didn't recognize and the girls were whispering quietly with a young couple, a woman angling for the empty seat to Faye's left asked to take it and then introduced herself to the two of us.

"I'm Helen Vance."

We both introduced ourselves.

"I'm sorry, you seem familiar but I just can't place you…" Faye said to her in a tone that was both curious and questioning.

"Oh, I'm sure you've seen me around. Sheila and I grew up together in Zanesville. We've been friends for as long as we can remember. I live in Columbus now but we still try to get together as often as we can; often to hang out here. This is such a quaint little town."

Agreeing with her, I said, "I've just spent the week here and I'll certainly be back. It's so different from the Pittsburgh area where I live."

"Which is probably a lot like Columbus so, that it is. Hopefully now, I'll be welcomed here a little more often." Helen looked away from me and down at her plate rather abruptly.

Faye and I shared a look and then she prompted Helen, "Something kept you away before?"

"I'm here for Sheila today, poor soul. I've always been her friend and I always will be but I've never been a fan of his," the woman whispered. "Sometimes I just couldn't bear to come down here knowing I'd be spending time with not just her but him too."

Faye had no idea what to say; she simply raised her eyebrows in a look of surprise.

The woman seemed inclined to continue, "She deserved so much better," she whispered. "He wasn't abusive, not that I knew but, God rest his soul, he wasn't attentive either, not to her anyway."

"I'm sorry. Whatever do you mean?" Faye was still somewhat taken aback by the sudden brashness of the woman.

"I mean, there were other women. Let me tell you, Terry had a habit of sneaking off to Tennessee with other women… to meet with other women…would say he was going to his brother's to fish or hunt. Well Sheila caught him out one time and she decided to follow him down there when he said he was going to his brother's to confront him about it."

"Really? Well, whatever came of that?"

Now the other woman was out of steam. She shrugged, "I don't quite know what happened down there or whatever came of the whole situation but I do know that Sheila was actually back before Terry was. I was at my sister's house in Zanesville. She was over there in a flash, crying on my shoulder, she was!"

Viva Mama Rossi!

I excused myself to fetch a cup of coffee. When I returned, two men were standing at the end of the table talking with all of the Cranes. Faye introduced them to me as Terry's brothers, Pete and Steve Ford.

"Steve lives here locally Chloe, and Pete is up from Tennessee where Terry was originally from."

"My condolences to both of you."

"Thank you," the two men replied in near unison.

Jesse, looking at Pete, spoke up, "How've the whitetail been running?"

"It's been a good season so far. Terry didn't make it down for the first round of bow hunting and he really missed out. He was looking forward to coming down for the second round of bow season later this the month."

I watched Mel give Dana a look. *Now, what's that all about?* I didn't get a chance to ask as the two men moved on to speak with others and Mel stood up to excuse herself.

Faye eyeballed me, "Why don't you show me where you got that coffee? I could sure use a cup."

Once we were at the coffee urn and out of earshot of most of the mourners in the hall, Faye spoke quietly, "There's a lot of talk flying and a lot of stuff going on here that doesn't make any sense."

"Tell me about it!" I shook my head. "Everyone is either acting oddly or they have an axe to grind."

"It makes me wonder," Faye began, "If…"

"Pardon me, Faye, Chloe," Lucy Sharpe interrupted her. Faye turned to her, "Yes?"

"I just wanted to apologize for, well you know, before. I realize I was a little rude and that wasn't right."

"No harm done Lucy." Faye smiled, seemingly ready to forgive easily for the small transgression.

"It's just that I really talked out of turn the other day. I really shouldn't have said anything at all. I felt so bad after I spoke with Amy about it because she got a bit annoyed with me. She said it was all just a misunderstanding; Rich blew it out of proportion…"

"I see," Faye told the near tears shopkeeper. "Say no more. Consider it forgotten."

I nodded my own consent.

Lucy, seeming a little relieved, wandered back toward the food line where the other servers were beginning to clean up.

Faye looked around. A couple of dozen people were still milling about. She put her coffee down. "Let's go talk somewhere a little more private." She headed toward the restroom and I followed.

Once the door was closed, without preamble, Faye dived right in, "Now Lucy is acting even more strangely."

"It seems like she was feeling a little guilty about gossiping to me, especially after the object of her transgression dressed her down for it."

"No," Faye said, "I know Lucy and I know Amy. There's more that Lucy isn't telling us. I'll bet when she talked to Amy, Amy gave her an earful but not just a dressing down. Now it seems like she's backtracking, trying to defend Amy."

I didn't know what to say to that. Faye certainly knew the players better than I did.

Faye threw her hands up, "People are just coming out of the woodwork with bad things to say about Terry. First that

Helen woman with the stuff about Terry going to Tennessee all the time and Sheila catching him down there, then his brother stands right there and says he hasn't been there in a while; now this stuff with Lucy…I'm beginning to think Sheila might have actually pushed the man into that pond and held him under!"

"I don't know that I'd say all that, now." I related the conversation I overheard about Art at the viewing to her. "There's more than one person out there that's not sad to see the man gone, I'm sorry to say. Give Sheila the benefit of the doubt here."

* * *

Mel

Gun belts are a pain in the butt for female cops when nature calls. I was standing in a toilet stall, minding my own business, trying to fasten mine back on in the tight space when I heard my mother and Dana's come into the restroom and immediately set their gums to flapping.

I didn't know what to do. It was obvious they thought they were alone and their conversation was certainly of interest to me so, like a brazen eavesdropper, I just stood there quietly.

Their chat didn't take even a minute but I learned more in that time than I had in several days of farting around with the Tennessee authorities. My gut now told me Sheila might very well have pulled the trigger on the shot that killed Patricia Dunkirk.

After waiting a couple of minutes, I slipped out of the

restroom and around to a stairway that would take me up and out towards the front of the sanctuary rather than through the fellowship hall and out to the parking lot. I felt confident that if either my mother or Chloe were still in the hall, I wasn't spotted leaving the restroom.

* * *

Mel

Saturday Evening, October 17th, 2014
The Boar's Head Bar

Chloe had the house well under command. She'd decided, after talking to Mario back in McKeesport, to go ahead and stay on for another week, at our request. While I went back to work, she and Dana were going to go shopping for a dining set and some living room furniture among other things plus whatever the 'dog to be named later' needed.

I was still refusing to call the puppy 'Boo' but I think my wife was undermining my desire to have it named anything but that.

Dana and I took the night off since we were still technically supposed to be on our honeymoon. We were relaxing at the Boar's Head, the bar owned by a former ex-girlfriend turned enemy then friend, Barb Wysocki. There was a country western band playing on the little stage near the newly installed dance floor and the place was jumping with a mixed crowd of fall foliage tourists and locals all out enjoying a warm fall Saturday night.

We'd ordered food that Barb brought out herself. We invited her to join us.

"Don't mind if I do ladies. My crew can handle this crowd just fine for a few minutes." She took a seat.

"You've really turned this place around. The difference is amazing," I told her.

Barb smiled, "I won't say it's been easy. It hasn't, but it's been more fun than I expected. Continuing to do this was a difficult decision to make after my partner died."

"If you've transformed all the places you've taken over like you've transformed this one, you've done really well despite your loss," Dana told her. "The struggle seems to bring out the fire in you."

"Thank you for that. Yes, you're right. It does keep me busy and keep me going when my mind gets to wandering."

I was curious, "Will you stay Barb? Now that this one's pretty much done, I mean?" I asked her.

"You know the deal is 'turn and burn' right? I know I told you that."

"You also told me once that you keep ownership of a few places for the revenue to buy and flip other places, right?"

She laughed. "That's why you're such a good cop. You have a memory like a steel trap. Yes, that's what I said and yes, I'm keeping this particular bar in the portfolio."

"But you're not going to stay on, are you?" Dana asked.

Barb leaned into the table, "A secret, just between the three of us…well, and my banker…I'm tired of life on the road. I put an offer in on a house a couple of days ago and the seller took it."

Dana said, "That's awesome!" through gritted teeth as she tried to not look too excited and arouse attention.

"Barb, that's great! Where?" I asked her, whispering just loud enough to be heard over the bands current ballad.

"It's a place Aiden Quinn bought several years back and renovated. I think he thought one of his kids would live there one day but none of them have showed any interest. They all think the grass is greener outside of Morelville. Anyway, I'll have a couple of dozen acres but he keeps the mineral rights. I don't care about those anyway. I'm comfortable with what I have now."

"If it's the place I'm thinking of, we'll practically be neighbors."

She confirmed the location I suspected and then I described the house there for Dana's reference. Once I'd divulged some of the features it, Dana recalled seeing the house in question and she became even more excited for Barb. "When do you close?" she asked her.

"Pretty quickly. Probably in the next couple of weeks. It's an all cash deal so his lawyer is drawing it up for mine to look over." She sighed.

"That doesn't sound so good..."

"No, really, I'm very happy about it. I've lived on the road for so long though that it's just, *well*, I have a storage unit near Detroit, my last stop, that's full of modern steel and glass stuff. It never really was my taste and it's not a fit for this place at all."

"Oh Barb, do we have the perfect person to help you!" Dana couldn't contain her excitement. Dana and I looked at each other and laughed.

"Sounds like Mama Rossi could have a new assignment when she's done with our place…"

"Mama Rossi?"

"My mother Chloe, Barb. You met her at the wedding reception last week…she hasn't actually left. Instead, she's been trying to put a dent in my wallet by furnishing our place for us."

"Really? Do you think she'd help me?"

"I'll ask but I don't see why not," Dana replied. Can your wallet take it?"

"Oh, money isn't an issue. But, will she work with me on styles?"

"She's done fine by us but we're both okay with the rustic wood look and she knows that. You'll probably want to hang with her the first couple of shopping trips until she gets a feel for what you like."

"What does she charge as an hourly rate?"

We both laughed but Dana recovered first, "Our bank account, our patience, the use of our kitchen, putting up with fussy little dogs…take your pick." Dana coughed. "In all seriousness, she's not a professional decorator, if that matters. She's a trained nail tech and that's what she does for 'pin money', as she calls it. You'd have to work out any sort of payment arrangement with her but don't be surprised if she refuses anything but expenses."

As Barb nodded, the country/western band stopped playing on the little stage on the other side of the room and announced a set break. She stood up. "I best get behind the bar. Their breaks always mean everybody's off the dance floor, thirsty and crowed around up there."

After she walked away, I asked Dana, "You're okay with her moving so close and your mother helping her if she's willing, right?"

"Of course. Why wouldn't I be?" She squeezed my hand briefly. "Mel, I know there's nothing between the two of you. Frankly, she's still in mourning and she always seems so depressed. Maybe once she settles down, she'll feel up to finding someone new."

"Don't ever say that to her babe. You can't push Barb to do anything she doesn't want to do. She's changed a little over the years but I still see flashes of that stubborn streak in her that so irritated me way back when."

Dana smirked at me but I didn't want to know what she was thinking.

While she gloated, the group sitting at the table next to us got up and left. Just as fast, a group of four local guys swooped in and took over the dirty table. They were faster than the server who was working her way over to it to clean it.

While she tried to clear off around them and their good natured ribbing, one of the guys, Chuck Knox, turned sideways and noticed me.

"Hey there Mel. How are you?"

"Fine Chuck, and you?"

He tipped his head side to side, "So-so; just out tonight doing a little send-off for my old buddy Terry. I'm going to miss him."

I nodded. "You two have known each other a long time, haven't you?"

"Ever since his family moved up here from Tennessee

when he was a freshman in high school."

"Helluva way to go," one of the other men said. I didn't recognize the guy.

"You don't have to tell me! I feel bad about that every day!" Chuck's head dropped.

"Chuck, he drowned. It wasn't your fault," I told him.

"He drowned in my pond Mel. If only I had been there. He usually fished that pond for bluegill with somebody else. I didn't know he ever worked his way out to that one alone."

"That's not something you could have helped, Chuck," the man who'd spoken before told him.

"Stop beating yourself up about it," I added. There were nods all around the guys table. The server finished clearing and asked the men if they wanted anything. They ordered a round of drinks for themselves and included refills for me and Dana.

"Just one, Chuck," I said, "for my dad, in Terry's memory." Dad had stopped drinking at mom's request several years back. I'm sure they'd invited him out tonight and just as sure that he'd told them no.

When the server returned with the drinks, Dana and I stood near their table while Chuck raised his glass. "A toast to Terry Ford. Rest in peace old pal and make sure you keep the tall tales under your old fishing hat."

Everyone grinned and swigged their beverage of choice. A man who looked vaguely familiar to me said, "The fish in the fish stories are going to be a little smaller around here now." There were nods among all the men.

Dale Walters, who hadn't been at the funeral or the wake that I'd noticed, spoke up and said, "And the poker pots will be just a little bit bigger." Chuck shot Dale a look but the other two men nodded their agreement.

I was about to politely excuse myself and Dana when cranky old Art Majors stepped up to the men's table.

"Why so glum, everybody?" he asked the assembled men.

"We were just drinking a toast to Terry, Art," Chuck told him.

Art waved his hand in the air like he was swatting a fly. "Hell, fishing around here will be a lot more 'honest' now that Terry's gone."

Chuck looked annoyed but the man I didn't know at all jumped on Art's comment and ribbed him right back, "At least he caught fish pal. You've been casting for pond scum lately."

"That may be so, but I just picked up a sweet reel that I can't wait to try with one of my rigs. I'll be up at Dillon next weekend if anyone wants to come up and have a little bass hooking contest."

No one responded. Art, seemingly at a loss for anything else to say, shrugged and said, "Have it your way." He took his leave of the table.

CHAPTER 19

Family Fun Day

Mel
Sunday, October 18th, 2014

Dana's dog was bouncing up and down beside the bed on my side. The room was still dark. Squinting at the clock, I saw it was only 4:35.

"Dana, your dog needs to go outside," I mumbled to her. No response came from the other side of the queen bed we were currently using. I stretched a foot behind me. I touched cool sheets, not warm legs.

Rolling over, I reached for her but she wasn't there. A thin glimmer of light shone from the bathroom.

I got up and walked toward the door then tapped gently so I didn't startle her. When she didn't respond, I pushed the door open. Dana was lying in the big soaking tub, fast asleep. Walking in and touching the water, I realized she must have been in the tub for a while. It was only lukewarm.

I called to her gently and woke her. "How long have you been in here?"

"What time is it?" She tried to stretch splashing a little water out. The pup, who'd followed me in there, didn't like the water much and ran back out.

"Just past 4:30."

"I couldn't sleep and you were out cold. I didn't want to wake you so I thought I'd soak a while. What are you doing up?"

"The dog is bouncing around like she's on a pogo stick. We should probably get a kennel for her to sleep in at night."

"She probably has to pee. Help me out of here and I'll get dressed and take her outside."

"I'll help you up but I'll take her out."

After helping Dana out of the tub, I walked back into the dark bedroom to find it strangely quiet. In the dimness, I stepped down on something that probably shouldn't have been in the middle of the floor in the dark and hurt my foot. While I hopped about, rubbing out the unexpected pain, I stepped into a puddle with my good foot of what could only have been dog pee and I cried out.

Dana yelled from the bathroom, "What's wrong?"

"Nothing. I don't think your dog needs to go out after all."

"Mel, you said you were going to do it!" She walked into the room.

I hobbled over to the bedside light and turned it on. Pointing back at the puddle, I said, "She already peed."

"My shoe!" Dana yelled again while looking at the floor near the foot of the bed. "My shoe! Bad dog! Bad Boo!" 'Boo' cowered in a corner as Dana picked up and inspected a well chewed Nike.

"Boo!" I yelled, throwing my arms in the air and waving my hands like a scary monster in the direction of the dog. She whimpered and laid down. "Her name does fit her after all…"

Viva Mama Rossi!

"You don't have to scare her Mel!"

"*You* just yelled at her Dana!"

Dana exhaled heavily, "We both need to stop yelling at each other and at her. She's only a puppy. I'll get her a kennel *and* get better about taking her out. We *both* need to mind what she has the potential to chew on."

"Look, I'm sorry. You're not in this alone. I'll help you with house training her and getting her outside." I shook my head and looked over in the corner at her. "Despite my reservations, she is a cute little thing." The terrier had the nerve to seem to understand my basic show of affection for her by coming over, sitting at my feet and looking up at me expectantly.

"I think she likes you."

I just shook my head as I reached down and scratched hers.

Our early morning turned into a long one. We were in and out with a puppy who I think was thriving on the attention she was getting from us more than she actually needed to relieve herself. Going outside seemed to be more of a sniff fest for her than a time to potty. Still, we'd made an agreement so tiredly we both trudged on, trying to housebreak our new fur baby.

Around about 7:30, while we were slouched in wood chairs in what had once been meant as a dining room but would be more of a sitting room for us, Chloe came regally down the stairs behind a Little Lady bent on heading for the door.

"We're so sorry mama; did we wake you?"

"No, no sweetie," Chloe said, waving a hand at her daughter. Lady always gets me up about this time. Besides, I'm going to church with Faye this morning and then after that, we're headed out to the farm for a 'Family Fun Day' as your mom called it," she said as she looked at me.

Dana and I both groaned.

"What's wrong with you two?" Chloe asked.

"There's nothing fun about family fun day!" we both told her, in unison.

"Kris and Lance are coming back from their honeymoon this afternoon since they couldn't change their flight in time to come in for the funeral. The kids are excited. Your mom," she pointed at me this time, "thought it would be nice to all get together for a family dinner to check in with each other."

I just nodded. It wasn't worth trying to explain it to her. She'd learn the truth about 'Family Fun Day' soon enough.

"Mel and I will meet you out there later this morning mama. We have several things we need to take care of first."

"So, you're not going to church then?"

Dana's look was sheepish but her reply firm, "Not this time. Sorry."

* * *

Mama Rossi

Faye and I sipped coffee in the fellowship hall after the service while she introduced me to different people here and there. The congregation represented a slightly smaller slice of the community than was present at the funeral service the day before and, as I suspected might be the case, everyone really did seem to know everyone. Try as I might, at my church back in McKeesport, it just wasn't possible to learn all the names but that didn't seem to be a problem here.

"Oh, Chloe, this is Amy Johnson. Amy, this is Chloe Rossi, Dana's mother."

The woman took my hand and smiled slightly but the smile didn't seem to reach her eyes.

My ears perked up anyway, "Nice to meet you Amy." I did my best to sound sincere and cordial. Faye took it from there though.

"Were's Rich, hon? I thought I saw him during communion."

"He's upstairs talking with the Council President about the Fall Festival."

Faye caught my eye and tipped her head to the side, toward a back corner of the hall. Taking Amy's arm, she tugged her slightly toward the area she'd indicated. Once we were safely away from most of those reveling in coffee and cookies, she said to the younger woman, "Amy, I don't mean to be forward, what I do mean to do is apologize and try to smooth any feathers that may have gotten ruffled recently." Faye gave her what I took to be a sympathetic look.

"You don't have anything to apologize for Faye. Don't even think about it."

I heard her words, but her tone didn't match. Diving in myself, I tried to be diplomatic, "Faye and I were out doing some shopping and we were chatting with Lucy about... well, you know. Our conversation was brief, completely in passing and only between the three of us. Lucy really feels badly about mentioning anything at all and we feel horrible about even thinking to gossip, Isn't that right Faye?"

Faye nodded along with me.

"So," I went on, "please don't take it out on poor Lucy. We started it and the buck ends with us."

"Oh," Amy sighed, "If only it were that simple."

At our quizzical looks, she leaned forward into our tight little circle, "The thing is, I don't know how Lucy found out. Word seems to be spreading and I don't know who's saying what to whom or how much they really know." She hung her head.

Faye reached forward and touched the woman's chin gently nudging her. As Amy looked back at Faye, I could see the glimmer of tears shining in her eyes.

We were standing next to the closed door of the nursery. Nudging it open, Faye peered inside and then, satisfied that it was empty, beckoned the two of us in. She shut the door firmly behind us.

Spying a tissue box on a changing table, I grabbed it and offered it to Amy. She took one and dabbed at her now brimming eyes.

Faye hugged the younger woman briefly then took one of her hands and, looking her in the eye, prodded her, "Please tell us what's wrong dear. Get it off your chest and let's see if we can help you."

Amy took a deep breath as she tried to steady herself. Failing, she lowered herself instead into one of the tiny but sturdy chairs meant for rough and tumble toddlers bent on climbing and jumping and doing everything else that toddlers do. Faye and I pulled out chairs and followed suit.

"Rich travels a lot for work…a whole lot. What, with the

kids both in college now, I'm alone most of the time. I just hate…hate being alone. But, college is expensive and the money's good when he's on the road so away he goes…"

"Honey," Faye cautioned, "you don't have to say anything else. Just let it go."

"No, no…I want to tell you this. You're right, I need to get it off my chest and move on."

We both nodded silently at her and just let her talk.

"Terry was a flirt, you know?"

Faye simply shrugged.

"He was. If Sheila wasn't around, he was merciless. If she was there, he'd tone it down only a little. I just blew him off most of the time."

Most of the time, eh? Here it comes…

"One time, when we'd had plans with my family for a family get together made for more than a month, Rich decided at the last minute to take an optional short assignment that had him flying out the night before the party and returning the day after it. He ruined everything we'd planned and we had quite a row about it but, in the end, he went on the assignment anyway."

Amy dipped her head and rubbed her temples then she continued, "I was so angry with him, after he pulled away and headed toward the airport, I slammed out of the house and went for a walk. It was only after I got back that I realized the door had locked behind me and I had no keys with me. I didn't take my cell either. I walked over to the store and asked Terry to use his phone to call my sister and have her come down with her spare key."

"My sister didn't answer. Terry was minding the shop

alone and he invited me to stay until I got in touch with someone. He flirted non-stop, he said he was trying to cheer me up. For over an hour I tried to get a hold of Judy but I never did. In the end, he closed up the store and he went with me to help me break into my own house."

"We just…it just…I never meant for it to happen. I was just so mad at Rich and frustrated with myself and…"

"Stop, stop dear. It's okay," Faye told her.

I clucked my tongue, "You were vulnerable and he took advantage of you. It's not your fault Amy. It's not your fault at all, don't you see?"

Tears streamed down her face. I picked the tissue box back up and offered her another.

"He asked to see me again. I told him no…" She trailed off and sighed. "I felt so guilty, I completely avoided the store and Sheila for weeks afterward. I never told Rich…I couldn't. He'd have been so hurt and so angry."

"I guess I was naive to think some sort of word wouldn't get around, especially after Rich laid in to Terry…"

I was confused. "You just said you never told Rich…"

Amy shook her head vigorously and waved her hands in front of her, "Oh, no, no. I didn't. I was quiet about that and I avoided the store and anywhere that I might encounter Terry for a couple of months after it happened. But, one day, Rich and I were off doing something and on the way back we decided to grill burgers for dinner. Rich pulled in at the store and sort of gave me instructions to grab buns and chips while he grabbed a couple of other things."

"When we walked in, Terry wasn't up front. Rich went around to the back aisle, while I got my stuff off the front one. Terry must have heard the bell over the door jangle because he came out of the office and immediately saw me. He didn't realize Rich was there. Actually, I'm certain he thought we were alone because he started right in on me with 'Hey, I haven't seen you for a while,' and it got pretty lewd from there. When Rich realized he was talking to me, he came around the end of the aisle and he *blew up*."

Faye was sitting nodding at Amy as she spoke. Now, she reached forward and took Amy's hand in hers, "That might be all anyone knows about dear. I don't think you need to worry anymore…"

"I'm not sure what Rich knew then or what he knows now but I've been faithful to him since that day…and…and, up until that day."

I told her, "It's over. It's done. It doesn't do anybody any good to bring it all up again now that Terry is dead. Just let it be."

As we were driving out to the farm, Faye and I were talking. "I know Rich Johnson pretty well. If I was a betting woman, I'd be willing to bet that he probably knows more than Amy thinks he does."

"Amy knows him too Faye. Don't you think she'd sense if he was onto her?"

"He may be biding his time, waiting for her to come clean to him or maybe he's even waiting for the right moment to use it against her."

"You're right, I don't know him so I can't speculate. It sure makes things complicated though."

"What things?"

"Figuring out who may have wanted Terry dead. There are several people that we've run across now, besides Sheila, that disliked the man pretty intensely or who had a score to settle with him. We can add both Rich and Amy to the list."

* * *

Mama Rossi
The Crane Family Farm

"Chloe, you're about to experience a Crane family fun day. It's a Sunday tradition once or twice a month when things need doin' around here. That's why we went to church early. We've got cooking to do!"

"Whatever happened to Sunday being a day of rest?"

"Not on a farm sweetie, not on a farm…"

We cooked liked two crazed Army chefs readying to feed a battalion while Jesse, Mel, Dana and Kris's teenage children Beth and Cole picked the last of the root vegetables from the garden, got it tilled up for the fall and did various other chores around the Crane spread.

Right around 4:10 Faye sent me to the porch to let everyone know that Mel's twin sister Kris and her new husband would be arriving back from their own honeymoon in Florida shortly; they'd called that were on the ground and en-route. I was also let everyone know that dinner would be ready within the half hour.

Kris and Lance turned into the long drive right about 4:15, as I was heading back into the house. *All* work stopped then. I stopped too and watched as Beth and Cole ran from the barn across a field to the drive to meet up with their mother and their new step-father before Lance's SUV even rolled to a full stop. It was obvious to anyone watching, they were excited to have them home and, I suspected, even more excited to see if presents for them were in the offing.

I heard Kris exclaim, "I'm happy to see you both too… now let me get out of the car!" She and Lance lumbered toward the house like people tired of sitting for hours. I held the door for them and welcomed them home since Faye was still busy in the kitchen. The two kids bounced in behind them like excited toddlers instead of the teenagers that they were.

After a long, food packed dinner with lots of chatter and laughter about the highlights of both honeymoons, the kids ran off to do the things farm kids do in the dimming autumn light and we adults rolled ourselves fat and happy to the front porch for some more adult conversation.

Kris looked at her father critically, "You look good dad but how are you really feeling?"

Jesse just grunted at her and tried to wave her off but Faye was giving him the evil eye and he caught it. "I'm doing better. Those meds are a pain and I don't like to take them, that's what!"

"Dad," Mel cautioned, "those are what's helping your heart right now. You *have* to take them."

"I just said I don't like 'em, I didn't say I wasn't taking 'em."

"I worried about you a lot while we were gone." Lance

nodded in agreement with his wife.

"Don't be worrying about me," Jesse flipped a backhand at her, "I'm just fine."

"Whatever you say dad." Kris's tone was laced with exasperation. She looked back and forth between her mother and Mel, "So, which one of you is going to fill us in about Terry?"

Mel told her, "There's really nothing to tell. He fell into a pond he was fishing in out at Chuck's place and he drowned."

Jesse scoffed at that. Kris eyed her father but her mother spoke first, wresting her attention back toward her.

"I don't think it's quite that simple anymore Kris and your father never did."

Deferring again to her father, Kris asked him, "What do you think dad?"

Jesse, a man of few words, I was learning, thought for a minute as he worked his mouth to form the words. He finally spit out, "Didn't seem right to me. Just Terry and a pole. No bait, no tackle, wasn't wearin' his waders."

When he paused and didn't say anything else, Kris asked, "So Mel, you obviously disagree. What do you make of that?"

"I don't make anything of it. I wasn't here to see it but I trust my men when they say that they investigated the scene thoroughly but found no signs whatsoever of foul play and that's all I'm going to say about it."

"Well, I have a few things to say about the whole mess," Faye protested. "There's a lot going on surrounding it, if you ask me but, bottom line and heaven help her, I think Sheila may be involved somehow."

"Mom," Mel stuck a hand out to slow her mother's spew of speculation, "that's just not possible. Sheila was in the store that day at the time that he died and there are several witnesses that will attest to that."

"I still say she's involved somehow but maybe not directly. Terry was cheating on her. She actually followed him to Tennessee and caught him in the act and now he's dead and, God love her because I sure do, but she sure don't seem sorry about it!"

"They're just unfortunate coincidences mom."

I picked up on the word 'coincidence' right away and fired back at Mel, "There are lots of strange things going on all the way around his death, like your mother said, that even I can see from a layman's point of view. Why don't you explain what you mean by 'coincidences'?"

Mel sighed. She looked at Dana and then back at me. Twisting her head about to look at all of the group assembled on the porch, she said, "This doesn't leave this porch, got it?" The forcefulness in her voice had us all nodding vigorously.

"Dana and I found out that a woman Terry was apparently seeing was killed in Tennessee. The police there ruled her death a negligent homicide but we aren't so sure." Dana shook her head no, punctuating Mel's statement.

"The killer wasn't caught and the police down there were working under the assumption that it was a coyote hunter who fired an errant shot and never even knew what happened, when no one came forward."

"Mel's being charitable toward the Sevier County Sheriff's department," Dana supplied, "but I don't have to be. We did a little bit of investigating on our own and we *know* the woman was killed by an intentional shot from a .22."

Jesse jumped in, "You said they were thinking a coyote hunter done it?" At Mel's nod, he continued, "You don't hunt coyote with a .22!"

Mel responded to her father, "And you don't use jacketed rounds either. A hunter would know that."

My mind was whirling. Without really thinking it all out, I blurted "Sheila Ford has a .22."

"What?" came several responses.

"I was doing her nails before Terry's viewing on Friday. A .22 rifle leans in a corner by her kitchen door. I asked about it and Sheila told me Terry kept it there for groundhogs."

Mel asked us to just drop the subject and not say anything more about it so we did but I was positive I could see the wheels just turning in her mind.

CHAPTER 20

Boo Boo

Mel
6:15 AM Monday Morning, October 19th, 2014

I got into the office really early again but, this time, I didn't have a jump on Holly who had the whole place ship shape and was leaned back, pretending to file her nails when I arrived.

After a bit of ribbing from me and then a brief rundown of the personal side of my honeymoon, we got down to business. Holly was in tune with my thought processes and my habits. She knew I wouldn't have come in over the weekend or extra early this morning if I didn't think there was something pressing that needed attention.

"There's more that happened on our honeymoon that I haven't told you about," I began.

"Mel, I don't really want to know all the nitty gritty details, that's TMI territory right there, that's what that is."

"TMI?"

"Too much information."

"Oh…No, it's nothing like that!" I actually felt myself blush a little. *Cut it out right now! You're the Sheriff; you don't blush!* Holly grinned, adding to my pain.

Finally, taking pity on me, she said, "Relax. I know what you meant. What's going on?"

I quickly sketched out for her what had happened in Tennessee. She listened without comment until I was done.

"Those guys down there sound like pricks, pardon my French," she said and rolled her eyes.

"They're not my concern any longer. Finding out if Sheila Ford was down there, gunning for Terry, for Dunkirk or for both of them is."

"That's going to be a tough one Mel."

"Probably not as tough as you think. I'll have Shane get on establishing a link between Ford and Dunkirk. There are certainly witnesses down there who could link them." I thought about the rental office folks and the server at Bennett's. "I need to get them linked locally too. Once we establish all that, I'll have our DA or even the state AG go to theirs. I'm done dealing with the Sevier County Sheriff's Department." *Bunch of yahoos…*

"Also, there's at least one person here who's already said Sheila went alone down to Tennessee and 'caught Terry' to my own mother. I haven't actually said anything to her yet but I have no qualms having my mom make a statement pointing out where that info came from." I smirked.

"None?"

"Not one!" We both laughed. "I know what you're thinking; if my mom ever really had to come in and make a statement we'd end up with the history of Muskingum County."

"Ain't that the truth!"

"Seriously though Holly, we need to get on this quick.

I need you to pull whatever info you can find on Patricia Dunkirk and give it to Shane. After that, we need to put our heads together and work up some warrants to get Sheila Ford's credit card and bank card statements for September and her cell records for then and we'll want to search her home, specifically for a .22 rifle or pistol and some jacketed rounds."

When I finished up with Holly, I called the Columbus crime lab to talk to Izzy about the Steirs' murder case. She was at her Monday morning meeting. I elected not to leave her a message. I figured I'd be hearing from her soon anyway.

***

Mama Rossi

Boston Terriers are smart little dogs. I'd had one myself when I was a teenager. I knew Boo would pick up fast but Dana and Mel didn't seem to be so sure. I vowed to myself to look into some obedience training classes for her.

The girls didn't have a phone book in their new house and I wasn't sure about the whole idea of using computers like they were so fond of so I went next door just after 8:00 and, thankfully, found that Kris was up after getting the two kids off to school.

"I'm so sorry to bother you this morning but I have a question for you…"

Kris smiled, "It's no bother at all. Come on in. Coffee?"

"Thanks, but not this time."

"What can I help you out with?"

"My Dana has just fallen in love with little Boo…"

"She's a cutie," Kris interrupted.

I nodded, "That she is, but Mel doesn't seem to be taking to her very well."

"Mel will come around Mama Rossi; don't you worry. She loves dogs…she's just used to having bigger dogs."

"That's fine but…well, I really want to give her no reason to be frustrated with Boo and I want Dana to learn to work with the dog too because I think it will be good therapy for her with her leg problems and all."

"So you're talking about some sort of training?"

"Obedience training to start with, yes. Do you have a place near here or know someone who does training?"

"I know a guy that trains hunting dogs but…obedience? I don't think he does that." She shrugged, "I could ask him for you."

I was skeptical, "How about a pet shop or a groomer? They'd probably know someone who trains dogs."

"There's both of those in Zanesville. I can get you some addresses."

Armed with the addresses of the one local pet shop and two dog groomers that were within reasonable driving distance, Dana, Boo and I set out for Zanesville just after 9:00.

Stopping at the closest groomer first, Dana put Boo on a leash but the she seemed to prefer being carried over walking after turning a fearful eye toward all the traffic moving about.

When we entered the shop, the whir of a dryer sent the

little dog climbing from Dana's arms to her shoulder like she was trying to get away via actual flight. "She really does need training," I remarked.

Dana picked her off her shoulder and cooed at her, "You're fine baby girl. Everything's fine."

"I'll be right with you," a young woman running a dryer over a standard poodle told us. While we waited and watched her and another woman work with dogs up on tables, the door opened again and a man I'd peg as a few years older than me or so strolled in.

The other woman, who was trimming a cocker spaniel, looked round at him. She smiled and said to the man, "He's almost done Mr. Majors. Give me just another minute."

Hmm, could this be Art Majors? What are the chances? I looked the man over.

Catching me looking at him, he half turned away as if he didn't want to be bothered by me or anyone else.

I turned to Dana who was looking at the man curiously. Unexpectedly, she spoke to him, "Nice to see you again, Art, is it?"

The man peered at her intently then shook his head. "I don't believe I know you."

"We met briefly last night. I was with Chuck and his group."

The man had the nerve to harrumph loudly and turn away. I mouthed, 'how rude', to Dana. She half shrugged and continued to love on Boo.

The young woman working with the standard shut off the dryer and let the dog down from the table. Holding a single finger up toward us, letting us know to 'wait one', she led the poodle through a door at the back of the shop and then reappeared without it. "I'm Shae; how can I help you?" she addressed us, her eyes on Boo. She smiled a genuine smile as she watched the puppy whose curiosity was now overcoming her fear.

Dana spoke up, "We're looking for some obedience training for this little girl right here. Can you recommend anybody we could work with?"

The man waiting for the spaniel harrumphed again, loudly this time. "Just train her yer'self like everybody else does."

"Now Mr. Majors," Shae cautioned him, "small breeds can be pretty feisty but they respond well to all sorts of training and purebred Boston's like she appears to be can even do advanced agility. They're very athletic."

"Well now isn't that something?" I looked first at my daughter. *They could do agility training together and both benefit from it…* When she didn't respond right away, I looked at Major's on her left who's eyes were now boring into Boo. "So you're Art Majors are you?"

Dana stared at me while the man himself grumbled, "I think we've already established that. What's it to you?"

"It's just that you were missed at the funeral for Terry Ford the other day, is all. Several people asked about you."

My daughter was giving me the evil eye but I plowed on, "As I understand it, you two were great friends once. It's a shame you didn't make it to his send off."

"Just who the hell are you lady?" He was angry now, his face red with his fury.

"Mama!" Dana was beyond annoyed. She gave me a

look that could only be read as 'shut up!'

"Can I have my dog please?" Majors demanded. "I don't come in here to get harassed by people I don't even know!"

The young woman working with the spaniel lowered the table and let him off of it, rang Majors out and sent him on his way with a 'thank you for your business' that he didn't even acknowledge.

When the door closed behind him, Dana addressed the two women, "I apologize for my mother." She shot me another look, "I don't know what's gotten into her!"

"No worries," Shae replied.

"Yeah, he's always grim and gruff," the lady who'd been working with Majors' dog told us.

While I got the name of a trainer and her number out of Shae, I had Dana have the other groomer trim Boo's nails and pay her, even though I could have done her nails myself. I just felt bad for stirring up trouble that Art Majors might take out on them. I even had Dana buy her own set of nail clippers from them. They were twice the price they would have been at a big box store but I knew she could afford it.

"What the hell was all of that about in there, Mama?"

"You don't have to shout dear."

"What are you trying to do?"

"Nothing at all. I was just making conversation."

"You call needling that man 'conversation'?"

"Okay, call it making an observation then, if that makes you feel better."

"You're crazy, you know that?"

* * *

Mama Rossi

I tried the number I had for the trainer but I got her voicemail. After leaving her a message, we headed back to the house. Dana was annoyed with me and we had Boo with us anyway so doing any furniture shopping was out of the question.

As soon as Dana was off in her room and out of earshot, I called Faye and told her about Art.

"I know him Chloe. He always has been a little rough around the edges but he's not usually rude…not to that extent, anyway."

"I may have been a little pushy…"

Faye laughed but then spoke in a more serious tone. "There are just too many people that we've heard about now that had something against Terry. Too many to believe his death was a chance accident, for sure."

"Your daughter is adamant that Sheila didn't kill him."

"Not directly but what if she had someone else do her dirty work Chloe?"

"Who? Dingy Dale? Art? Rich Johnson? Why would any one of them risk getting caught to off him just for her? What would be in it for them, in that regard? I think, if one of them were going to do it, it would probably be for his own reasons, don't you think?"

"Yeah, but which one?"

"That, I don't know."

"There has to be something Mel's deputies missed

Chloe…there has to be."

"I hear Dana stirring Faye, I better go…"

"Are you going to be right there?"

"Probably, why?"

"I'll be by in five minutes to get you."

We were in Jesse's truck again. "Where are we headed?" I asked Faye.

"The pond that belongs to Chuck Knox…where Terry died."

"You know where it is?"

"Sure; when I was a teenager, it was our swimming hole…me and my friends, that is. The Knox family didn't own it then. Chuck bought the property shortly after he got married and struck his first well."

"Is everyone in the oil business around here?"

"Oil or natural gas – lots of them are."

We drove for a few minutes down one dirt road then turned down another that was more dirt track than road and eventually reached a rather large pond set deep in the woods.

"What are we looking for out here?" I asked Faye.

"Something the police missed. Tackle stashed somewhere, for example. They didn't find any out here. Really though, it's been years since I've been out here. I just kind of wanted to get a feel for it…see what's plausible."

"It's really overgrown all the way around, except on this side." We were parked on the track along where we'd come into the area of the pond. Other than on this side, where it was fairly smooth over to the bank, there was no real clearing. Everything the rest of the way around was wooded and, in some areas, thick with brush.

"There's barely enough clear area on this side to turn a vehicle around. It doesn't seem like Terry would have wandered far from here."

We got out of the truck and walked over to the bank. The still water of the pond was green with algae but not yet overrun with it. Other than the sound of a few crickets, it was eerily quiet in the area.

"It's changed a lot since I used to hang out here on summer afternoons," Faye said. Of course, it's technically posted as private property now. The family that owned the land back then had kids my age. Big groups of us hung out here. That kept the brush and the algae down."

The hair stood up on the back of my neck, "I'm getting an odd feeling Faye."

Before she could even form a reply, we heard a vehicle in the distance. We waited and watched. When it was obvious it had turned up the track to the pond, we retreated back toward the truck for a better view of whatever or whoever was coming.

"It's probably just Chuck," Faye said.

A pickup truck, driving slowly, finally came into view.

"Oh, oh. Not good."

"What? What isn't good?" I asked.

"It's Art Majors, of all people."

Now I shuddered. After our little dust up this morning, I didn't relish another meeting with the man. "What's he doing here?"

"He lives maybe a mile from here. He probably has permission to fish here too."

Art rolled to a stop. Instantly, his door flew open and he climbed down out of the truck and strode toward us. Anger flared in his eyes.

"I thought I saw somebody headed down this way. Just what the hell do you too think you're doing?" He started at Faye intently for a few seconds and then looked me over. "You again! I should have known your nosiness had something to do with this one," he jabbed a finger toward Faye."

We stood our ground but he wasn't backing down either. "You two have no business being out here."

Faye's temper flared, "You don't own the pond Art so back off. I'm just showing my friend here around."

Art grabbed Faye's arm. "You aren't fooling anybody," he said. "You're just out here to stick your noses in where they don't belong! Look, Terry's death was an accident and it's better left that way."

Faye tried to shake her arm loose from his grasp. Failing she said, "You let go of me right now Art Majors or I'll report you for assault and have Mel look at you real close."

"For what? For telling you that you two are crazy? Terry's dead. It wasn't murder; now drop it and move on and let the rest of us move on too."

He released Faye and we both scrambled into the truck. Before he could even get seated inside his, Faye was maneuvering Jesse's Ford to get around Art's, nearly taking off his still open door in the process, the maneuvering room was so tight.

Majors recovered and got his own vehicle turned around quickly. He followed us back down the dirt track and then onto the dirt road. I shot nervous glances at Faye as she white knuckled the steering wheel.

When we hit the paved road and turned to head to the right, I saw Faye breath a visible sigh of relief when Majors went left. "He must be headed back to his house," she said.

Faye took us to the farm. When we pulled up, Jesse was standing there watching us climb out of his truck.

"You look like you've seen a ghost. Where 'ya been?" he asked his wife.

We told him all about what happened.

Rather than being sympathetic to our plight, Jesse took Art's side. "Art and Terry were close until, in Art's mind, Terry double crossed him. Terry was Art's only close friend. Art's been lonely since he stopped paling around with Terry and now that Terry's gone, there's no chance to make amends. The man is just feeling sorry for himself. You two just need to leave well enough alone."

"Jesse," Faye pleaded, "you had to see the man. He was on fire."

"I don't want to hear any more about it, now. Art can be a handful but he would no sooner hurt a flea than hurt Terry, no matter how mad at him he was."

Jesse turned to me, "I have an errand to run. Hop back in and I'll run you into town."

He started around the truck without waiting for an answer. I looked at Faye. She just spread her hands in defeat. I got back into the dusty Ford.

Our short ride into town was a quiet one. As far as Jesse was concerned the case was closed. I wasn't so sure.

Viva Mama Rossi!

Did Art come out there just to run us off? Why? He wasn't intending to fish...he didn't have a fishing pole or any bait or tackle that I could see when we passed by that truck of his getting out of there. What's he up to?

CHAPTER 21

Trash or Treasure

Mama Rossi
Tuesday Morning, October 20th, 2014

"Hi Chloe; Dale Walters from Dale's Curios. That dry sink is ready to go, finally. I apologize for it taking a little longer than I expected but it's done now and you can come and pick it up any time. We're open until 5:00 today. Thanks. We look forward to seeing you."

In all the hubbub over Terry's death and his funeral and such, I'd completely forgotten about the dry sink. It hadn't even occurred to me that it was supposed to have been ready on Friday.

I looked outside and saw that Mel's truck was in the driveway. *She must have driven Dana's car to work…*

"Dana?" I called out from the doorway between the kitchen and the future sitting room, then waited for a response.

"Yes mama," she answered from somewhere upstairs. I heard footsteps moving toward the top of the steps and then down until she made the turn and stood on the landing where she could see me.

"Sorry to pull you away from whatever you're working

on but, while I was running Little Lady out the guy from a shop just up the road called my cell and left me a message. He has a piece of furniture I ordered for the house ready for pickup. Can you drive Mel's truck?"

"Yeah, sure I can drive the truck but how big a piece of furniture are we talking about here? Do we need to take muscle with us?"

"They can help us load it there. It's not too big but it might be heavy for you and I to unload. We might want to wait till later for that."

Ten minutes later, we were pulling into the dusty, rutted little lot at Dale's shop. The look on Dana's face was completely skeptical.

"It's not as bad as it looks," I told her. "Trust me."

We wandered inside. The dry sink was sitting near the register area with a little, hand-lettered 'sold' sign on it. It looked great.

"This is what we're here for," I told my daughter as I ran a hand lovingly across the smooth top. It's called a dry sink. I thought it would look really nice in the kitchen in that empty corner, under the window."

Dale appeared from the back while Dana looked it over. She was all smiles as she finished her inspection. "It's very nice. I think you've hit a home run with this one Mama. It will look perfect in that corner."

Dale introduced himself to Dana while I silently patted myself on the back. I whipped out my bank card to pay the tab but Dana was hearing none of it. She paid for it herself after throwing on another $50 over Dingy's original quote because she felt, as I did, that the piece and the work he put into it were worth more than what Faye had practically browbeaten out of the man.

Dana helped Dale wrestle the sink onto a dolly then, while she went out to back Mel's truck up to the loading dock, he and I tried to maneuver it through his jam packed store to the stockroom.

"Whatever made you bring that all the way out into the shop?" I asked him, already frustrated with the effort.

His reply was sheepish, "I actually worked on it out here the night before last because I couldn't get it back into the back with all the other projects I had to clear out late last week. The wife's getting a little annoyed with all my mess, you see."

I can definitely see why... To Dingy, I just nodded.

As we worked the sink through the door into the back area, Dale surprised me with his question, "Was that you and Faye I saw yesterday out the road near the turn off for Knox's pond?"

"Yesterday? It could have been us out running around. Why do you ask?" My hackles rose but I did my best to keep them in check and to not sound too curious at the same time.

"Oh, I was just out there making a delivery...you know, out that way, and I thought it odd that you ladies were way out there too, is all."

"I think it odd that you make deliveries and you neglected to tell me that." I gave him a stern look.

"I wasn't doing a uh, a *shop* delivery, see. It was, uh, a personal trip for a, uh friend." He licked his lips nervously and his eyes darted about, trying to focus anywhere else but on me.

Pam appeared through another door and greeted me. With her present, Dale abruptly stopped talking and started shifting the dry sink toward the loading ramp and the waiting pickup.

"You should have told me we have customers Dale."

He peered back over his shoulder at his wife, his cheeks tinged red. "It's no big deal. It's just a pick-up…already paid for."

On our way back to the house, Dana remarked, "You really have quite an eye Mama."

It made me happy to hear her say that and I blushed a little but I tried to be modest, "Thank you sweetie. I try."

"I've been meaning to talk to you about something…run it by you."

"What's that dear?"

"You can say no and there'll be no hard feelings…"

"How can I say no when I don't even know what we're talking about?"

"I'm getting to that!" She shot me an exasperated look. "I'm just trying to figure out how to ask."

"Do you need something Dana?"

"No mama, it's not for me. It's for a friend of ours. Do you remember Barb, the woman who catered some of the food for the wedding reception?"

"Yes, Mel's old friend, right?"

"Right. Well, she's decided to buy a house in the area and move back here to stay. She's been moving around the country for a while but this is where she's from."

"And she wants my help for something?"

"She told Mel and me that she has some furniture from a house she had before but that it's not a fit for the style of this house. Wait; I'll show you."

Dana took a right on a side street a couple of short blocks up from her own house and pulled into the driveway of a home set back off the road a little ways but still plainly visible. "This will be Barb's new place."

"Wow! Very nice. Kind of a colonial style outside. What's it like inside?"

Dana shrugged. "I have no idea. She's buying it from one of the big shot oil guys around here and I hear it told he's into the rustic look but, this was never actually his home. It may be completely empty, even."

"What you're telling me is Barb wants help decorating?"

"Yes. Would you be interested; once you're done with our place, that is?"

"I do enjoy it, don't get me wrong but…well, I feel like I should get back to your father soon. The get-away has been wonderful but he's been left to fend for himself and then there's my nail clients, and your brothers, and my granddaughter…"

"Mama, it's okay. Just a thought, okay? Maybe, if you are actually interested, you could help out part time, sort of consult with her and come up every other weekend or something. She's not in a big rush or anything."

"That's a thought. I *would* enjoy it Dana." I was quiet for several long seconds as Dana reversed out of Barb's driveway and headed back up the street toward the village's main road. Realizing I should probably say something, I asked, "When does she need an answer?"

Dana glanced at me and then back at the road. "There's a little time. She's waiting to close on it. It's a private sale… just waiting for the lawyers to do their thing…could take a couple of weeks."

"Well then, that puts us into November. Is she really going to want to decorate over the winter? That could get ugly around here."

"Good question…I don't know."

"Maybe I should just talk to her. Feel her out on the whole thing." Dana kept her eyes on the road but I could see her smirk plain as day.

It was early so Kris hadn't headed into work for the afternoon shift at the gas station yet. While Dana went to round her up to help us get the dry sink into the house, I gave Faye a quick call.

In a rush, I told her I only had a minute and I relayed what Dale had told me about being out making a delivery. Faye listened without comment.

When I finished and she'd still said nothing, I asked, "Do you think he might have something to do with Terry's death after all? I mean, would he really push him in the drink, all over a deer or even over the poker stuff he told us about?"

"It's doubtful dear. Dingy is capable of a little anger but I don't think he'd ever be physically violent with another human being."

"Well what could he be hiding then?"

"I'd think it's obvious; he's having an affair. Terry Ford wasn't the only cheater in town, you know."

CHAPTER 22

Ah Ha Moments

Mel
Wednesday Morning, October 21st, 2014

Shane and I were sitting in my office, combing through Sheila Ford's bank and cell phone records for anything that would show she was in Tennessee on Saturday, the 6th of September, the day Patricia Dunkirk died.

We'd jumped through some hoops to get the kind of cell records we had that showed global positioning, quickly. It didn't take me any time at all to find out there was a call made from her number that bounced off a tower in southern Kentucky early that Saturday that would have been near the route both Sheila and Terry would have likely taken.

Shane held up a bank statement, "They have a joint checking account and Sheila has a separate credit union account. This is the joint statement." He laid it in front of me and pointed, "It shows a filling station purchase, probably gas given the amount, in northern Tennessee that could have been made by either of them if we're still figuring the timing of their departures from home as being less than an hour apart." The look on his face was more a question than a statement.

"You know as much as I do on that score. I talked to

Helen Vance yesterday, the woman my mother talked to at Terry's funeral. She wasn't a lot of help. It seems that Sheila did come crying to her but It was probably the afternoon of Sunday, the 7th because she insists it was 'broad daylight' when Sheila was there and that wouldn't have been possible given that Patricia Dunkirk was killed around 2:30 Saturday afternoon, according to the media reports from Tennessee. It's a seven hour drive back for Sheila with *no* stops. So, I can't even verify the time she got back let alone the time she might have actually reached "

"How much do we trust Vance not to say anything to Sheila Ford?" Shane asked.

"I don't. That's why I told her I was just trying to tie up some loose ends on Terry's death, to satisfy everyone that it was an accident and that Sheila couldn't possibly have done it. I just opened with her talking with my mom at the wake and that's how I knew that she knew Sheila."

"Smart. That's why you're the Sheriff." Shane smiled.

"I'm beginning to think that I'm the Sheriff because I was the only one dumb enough to step up when Sheriff Carter died…"

"That's not true and we both know it. You were always the best person for the job and now you're the duly elected one. If only you could get someone to step up and help me out at detective…not that I mind working with you, ya' know, but it's wearing me out."

I sighed. "I know Shane. I've talked to Treadway. He's not interested. Some of the younger guys with potential just don't have enough seasoning for my liking yet. Would it pain you if I looked outside; like, say, at other departments?"

"No ma'am! I'd rather have someone from somewhere else that's got the time on the street and wants it than someone who doesn't have the experience that will completely slow us down."

"Gotcha. Point taken." I dropped my head back down and continued to scan through the cell records. Nothing at all jumped out at me as out of the ordinary. There was only the one call to question out of pages of data. Nothing else for that day came from her phone outside of its home area.

I glanced through the text records…nothing. Sheila Ford apparently didn't spend much time texting. I aloud, to no one in particular, "Does anyone of that generation ever text?" Shane didn't pay me any mind.

"This is useless." I tamped my stack of records into a neat little pile as my detective looked glanced up and then back down at his own stack. "The cell call is circumstantial," I continued. "It could have bounced off that tower for any number of reasons. Without asking the filling station to pull their video – if they have it from more than a month ago – we have no way of knowing which one of them bought gas…" I dropped my chin in frustration.

"Not so fast Mel." Shane held up the credit union statement he'd been studying.

"What? What did you find?"

"Sheila purchased something at Wal-Mart in Pigeon Forge on the 6th."

Bingo! "But, what did she buy?" I tried to contain my excitement. We had her in the area.

"That, I don't know but I'm going to give them a call, give them this transaction date and number and find out."

"Yes Holly?" I let go of the intercom button.

"Shane Harding on line 2 Mel."

"Thanks." I punched the button. "Shane?"

"Binoculars."

"She bought binoculars?"

Shane shook his head, "Yep. She most certainly did. Those, *and* full metal jacketed .22 rounds."

"Check and see how that search warrant is coming along for the Ford residence, will you."

"Roger that boss."

I hung up with Shane and buzzed Holly back. "Holly, we just caught a break in the Tennessee case. Can you get me the DA? I'm going to have to go up the chain with this one."

CHAPTER 23

A Haunting We Will Go

Mama Rossi
Late Morning, Wednesday, October 21st, 2014
Crane Family Farm

"Chloe, I just think it's a wonderful idea. You really should do it," Faye practically gushed at me when I relayed to her that Barb Wysocki wanted some help decorating her new home. "You're doing so nicely with Mel and Dana's place, after all."

Dana grinned beside me at the kitchen table. "She really is. We're very pleased with everything she's done so far and, frankly, it's such a relief to me. Mel and I agreed that I'd take the lead with the decorating but, I admit, it really isn't my forte."

"Well, I gave it some thought overnight and I talked to my Mario this morning. I do think I'm going to try and work out some sort of arrangement with Barb. I need to get the girls house done first though and then I need to get back and juggle a few things at home before I can tackle that."

"We should get going on today's outing then; drink up," Faye said, as she waggled a finger around the table at our coffee cups.

"You two are just going to love Sugarcreek," Faye told us. "There's so much there that's handcrafted. You just can't get that in Columbus."

"Not in Pittsburgh either," I replied, "not without paying a pretty penny for it, anyway."

"Thanks for driving and for showing Mama and I the ropes, Faye. I never even heard of Sugarcreek."

"It's my pleasure. You'll love it and, honestly, I've really enjoyed spending time with both you and your '*Mama*', as you call her."

Faye glanced over at me beside her, riding 'shotgun', "I'm glad you're going to be coming around more. We've sure had our little adventures, haven't we Chloe?"

"Shhh," I told her but I couldn't help my grimace.

Dana might not have caught the look on my face but she latched right on to Faye's pronouncement, "Adventures? What adventures?" She leaned into the split between the front seats and looked at me with what I'd describe in my daughter as a mixture of confusion and apprehension.

"Nothing serious dear." I flipped a backhand up over the seat. "We just seem to keep running into people that don't seem to care that Terry Ford is dead."

"Or," Faye put in, "that wanted him dead."

"Now Faye, none of them really seemed to go that far," I chided her.

"You two don't still think Sheila had something to do with her husband's drowning do you? Remember what Mel said the other day. She said…"

Now Faye waved a hand in the air, "We know what she said Dana; it's just that…that, there's so much going on surrounding the whole thing and it just doesn't all add up, is all. I think if Mel knew everything we know…everything we've heard, she'd really give his death a much closer look but she just didn't want to hear it at all on Sunday."

Dana was quiet for a long minute.

"What are you thinking, dear?" I asked her.

"It's just, Mel told you the other day what we learned in Tennessee and, well, none of it seems to tie into anything that's happened here."

"She told us that woman was shot with a .22," I said. "I told her Sheila Ford has a .22 in her house. That actually ties things together pretty well if you ask me!"

"Mama, really? Do you have any idea how many people in this town…hell, in this *county* have a .22 in the house?"

I shrugged, "No."

"Well I'll tell you, it's a lot! Mel can't base a case on just that."

"So you don't think Mel will look into that or have anyone look at it at all," Faye asked while looking in the rearview mirror at Dana.

"It's doubtful ladies. If she looks at the rifle at the Ford place, she may as well ask to see every single .22 rifle or pistol in the county."

We started off in Sugarcreek at Andreas Furniture then we headed over to the Amish run Troyer's and then doubled back to Weaver's, another Amish run establishment. Along the way we visited a couple of antique shops and a quilt shop. By the time 2:00 rolled around we were exhausted but we'd finally found a proper living room suite that Dana loved and that she and Faye agreed Mel would love too. It was scheduled to be delivered Friday. In the meantime, we picked out a couple of nice pieces and some décor for the room the girls had decided would be a sitting room, lacking any other ideas for it, but it was still a bit of a puzzle.

Gratefully, tired and hungry, we all collapsed into chairs at the Dutch Valley Restaurant. Faye looked between Dana and me, "If you ask me about anything on the menu, I'm going to tell you it's good. I've never had a bad meal here and I've always eaten too much, so be forewarned."

I laughed. "You'll get no complaints from me!"

"Me either," Dana said. Mom and dad both like to eat and I inherited that. Mel's always getting on me about never being able to miss a meal."

Faye swatted at Dana, "As if it matters. Look at you. You're only just now starting to fill in a little after being laid up for so long."

It was Dana's turn to chuckle. "Actually, I think most of my recent gain, so to speak, is a result of our daily pancake house visits in the Smokies. Your daughter is quite the pancake fan."

"That she is; don't I know it!"

The server appeared to take our drink order and pass out menus. She reeled off a list of fall specials that even included drinks like mulled cider and desserts like pumpkin and hot apple pie.

"I just love fall; it's my favorite time of year. The food, the views, the crisp air…It's pretty at home but I've really been enjoying being here today," I sighed and shook my head a little wistfully.

"Well now that makes me think of Barb again, Chloe. When does this project start?"

"The girls said she wouldn't be closing for a couple of weeks. That puts us into late October, early November before the place is officially hers."

"I agree that fall is beautiful here but the winter can be brutal. Colder temperatures are just around the corner and don't be surprised to see a little snow in mid-November or so. We're just inside the snow belt and it seems to be attracted to all these little valleys around here."

"If you're wanting to get started, you'll certainly want to plan to be around for the Fall Festival in a couple of weeks but you might want to consider leaving most of the heavy work for her for late spring."

I hopped right on the mention of a fall festival. "When's the festival and what's that all about?"

"What she really wants to know Faye," Dana interrupted, "is, will there be food?"

Faye laughed. When she regained her composure, she said, "You bet there'll be food and music and a haunted house and lots more."

Dana leaned into the table excitedly, "A haunted house?"

"You bet. They do one every year and every year it gets a little bit scarier. They're getting pretty good at it."

"Who's they?" I asked her.

"For the festival as a whole, the community, actually. There's a community center in the old school building. I'll have to take you up there."

Faye paused and appeared to think for a minute then she continued, "The fall festival has been around as far back as I can remember, kind of like the spring Mushroom Festival, but the haunted house has only been going about 5 years. That's a fundraiser for the center itself. The rest of the money they take in, like for food sales and such, goes back into the community for other things. Since Morelville is an unincorporated village, sometimes the difference between getting something done and not getting what we need is the money we raise ourselves. People come from all over for the fall fest and the haunted house."

"That haunted house idea sounds really cool," Dana picked the conversation back up after we placed our order. "I love those and I'd love to be involved. Who do I talk to?"

"Really? I never would have thought it," Faye replied.

"She gets it honest, Faye. Her father and brothers are huge fans too. Her dad is in the Jaycees. Back home, they do a house every year as a fund raiser. All the kids have been involved."

"Is that so? Well then, they're having their final planning meeting for the Fall Festival at 6:30 tonight. Most of the main players for the haunted house end of it will be there… heck, most of the town will be there. I planned to go because I'm usually involved with the food. Why don't you come along?"

"It's a date!" Dana beamed.

"Make that three," I added. I'd like to go too. If Barb wants me to get started before the snow flies, I'm probably going to be around more than I thought in the next month. I have both 'make-up skills and cooking skills."

"Makeup?" Faye asked.

"Gory makeup," I told her. "You don't think Mario puts on his own face, do you?"

CHAPTER 24

Seized

Mel
Wednesday Evening, October 21st, 2014

It took most of the day but we finally got the warrant to search the Ford residence. The DA, Tyler Whitesell, ran the info I gave him up the flagpole to the Attorney General. The AG was, I hoped, coordinating with the Tennessee authorities.

Unfortunately for the Tennessee folks, I still had the round I'd dug out of the wall in the cabin and even the shell casing I'd found. We'd do the testing of the rifle here, if we found it in Sheila's home; the DA vowed to see to that. I didn't want the bumbling excuse of a Sheriff's department down there to go anywhere near the evidence Dana and I had collected.

I called Dana late in the day to tell her I'd be stuck at work a while longer and not to worry. I was hoping to sneak into Morelville with a search team without her even knowing what we were up to. It wasn't that I expected her to blab; far from it. I just didn't know how she'd take having to sit out something she'd been a part of from the start.

My worry had been needless; before I could even offer an excuse, Dana let me know about the Fall Festival

Meeting. I knew, but Dana likely didn't, that Sheila sat on the Community Center Board. She, if she was up to it, would be at the meeting too which gave us a prime opportunity to conduct our search while she was out of her house and most of the town was otherwise occupied.

Shane Harding and Joe Treadway rode in my county SUV with me. Two other Deputies followed in cruisers and a forensic unit from the Columbus crime lab brought up the rear. My old buddy Izzy wasn't the tech rolling with us but I knew the one who was, Laura, and I knew she was more than competent to do the job. Still, I made a mental note to call Izzy in the morning about the Steirs case that was still pending fingerprint analysis.

We rolled into Morelville, past the gas station. Kris was on duty working her usual shift and, because she happened to be outside unlocking the propane cage when we drove through, she spied our little caravan immediately. I didn't acknowledge her wave and I prayed that her customer, a man I didn't recognize that was there apparently to buy propane, wouldn't have a clue what we were about.

I pulled my truck right into the Ford driveway behind Terry's old pickup and Sheila's car. The two cruisers parked out along the road, allowing the crime lab vehicle to pull in behind me.

"Sheila Ford may be here," I said to Harding and Treadway. "The sedan is her primary vehicle. I don't consider her dangerous."

We all dismounted and gathered in the driveway. I strode up the side porch steps I knew the Fords' typically used and rapped on the door. There was no answer.

I knocked again and called out, "Sheila Ford, police. We have a warrant." There was still no reply.

Treadway stepped forward, "Should we ram it Sheriff?"

"It's Morelville Joe; let me try it first." He nodded and backed down a step so I could move out of the way and swing the door open.

Out of habit, I unlatched my holster and put my hand on the butt of my service pistol but I didn't draw it. I reached across with my left hand and opened the screen door then, holding that open with my right hip, I tried the knob of the entry door. It opened easily.

Swinging the door into the interior of the kitchen slowly, I called out to anyone listening again, "Sheila Ford? Sheriff's Department, we have a warrant." Again, there was no response.

I stepped into the kitchen. Joe and Shane followed immediately behind me. Looking back toward the door, I wasn't surprised to see the .22 rifle right where Chloe had said it would be. I pointed that out to Shane who called the crime lab tech in. While Laura photographed that and then put gloves on so she could collect it, the three of us cleared the house. No one was there.

After calling the rest of the search team inside, I gathered them for quick instructions. "We're not tossing this place, got it?" There were nods all around. "We're specifically looking for any other .22 caliber weapon that might be here, binoculars and any .22 caliber rounds that you can find – Jacketed or not, box or no box. We're also authorized to take any computer equipment or external drives found and some other things, as applicable. If you see something else that seems relevant, don't touch it. Call me or call Harding over to review what you've found. Everyone got that?" I got another round of nods out of the assembled deputies and then I assigned them to rooms.

"No round in the rifle Sheriff. It's just a single shot," Laura told me.

"Thanks," I nodded and walked out of the kitchen, thinking to myself, *What's the point of keeping a loaded gun by the door if it isn't loaded? Where did the round that should have been in it go?*

It wasn't long before Joe handed over a loaded .22 caliber revolver he'd found in a nightstand in the master bedroom. The crime lab tech cleared the cylinders of their unjacketed rounds, recorded them and the pistol and then bagged it all.

Later, I was in the den with Shane as he went through Terry's desk. Store records were piled all over it and every other available semi-flat surface. Terry's filing system seemed to be no system at all.

There was no computer in sight but that didn't surprise me, even though the Ford's ran a retail store. The computer age had passed Terry's generation by and Sheila wasn't much younger than Terry had been. Internet service was expensive out here in the sticks and most of the older people in the village with no children at home didn't bother with computers or internet. *Hell, the cash register at the store is from the early days of the electronic age...*

Shane rifled through the papers on top of the desk and then started opening the drawers. When he pulled open the bottom of the three right side drawers he paused.

"Did you find something?"

"Maybe; there's a cell phone in here. He reached down with a gloved hand and pulled it out then held it out to me.

I didn't have gloves on so I didn't take it from him; I just looked at it instead. "It looks like the one Terry used to use."

"Could it be his most recent one?"

"I don't know for sure," I half shrugged.

"We didn't pull Terry's cell records Sheriff. That might come back to bite us if he has calls during the time of death that are not originating in ending up in that area of Tennessee. We should probably take this and at least check its call history."

"Do it. I'll get the DA on the line but I'm sure he'll tell me we can consider it computer equipment."

I called Tyler and let him know what we'd found while Shane continued his search. The den closet yielded a gun safe to him that was stashed in the very back, right corner with an ammo box sitting on top and then a small Sentry brand fire proof box on top of that.

"What do we do with all this?" His look was a little perplexed.

"We go through what we can. The fire box could be personal papers, valuables or even another pistol. The ammo box isn't sealed in any way, let's get the tech in here and have her go through that. I'll need to get the gun safe either removed or opened but, given what it is, we have the right to search it."

While Shane went to get the crime lab tech, I gloved up then pulled the fire box off the top of the stack and tried to open it. It was locked. I carried it over to the desk and set it down then went back for the ammo box. It wasn't very heavy. Without even looking in it, I knew it couldn't be more than half full. I toted that over to the desk too but ended up setting it on the floor while I moved some stacked paper out of the way.

Shane reappeared with the tech in tow. "Look what we have, Sheriff." Two sets of keys dangled from the fingers of his outstretched hand.

"His and hers?"

"Probably boss. I grabbed them when I saw the Sentry keys on them. We can at least get into the fire box without breaking it open."

"Let's do that first."

The tech stood by, camera ready, while Shane worked the lock. It popped right open. Inside was nothing but paper. I waited while Laura took a quick photograph then I scanned through the documents myself, "Marriage certificate, birth certificates, truck title…all the usual stuff. I don't see a will or any sort of death certificate for Terry though and I don't see any insurance documents for either of them. That's a little odd." I looked at the tech, "Did anyone else turn any of that sort of thing up?"

"No Sheriff."

Shane swung his arm around the room, "They're probably somewhere in these stacks." He dropped his head and shook it, "It will take days to go through all of this."

I sidestepped several inches to a position in front of the ammo box. "First things, first." Before I could even lift the lid though, the house phone rang. There was a receiver in the office but I didn't bother to pick it up.

After four rings, the ringing stopped. I lifted the lid on the box and looked inside to see two boxes of shotgun shells and a handful of loose ones on the top. The tech took a picture and then I reached in to remove the boxes.

One of my deputies stuck his head around the door frame, "I'm still working the kitchen Sheriff. A woman named Molly left a message on the machine just now asking if everything was okay. She sees all of the police vehicles down here."

Shane looked at me, "What do we do boss?"

"Molly's the busybody Postmaster. It's a wonder she's not got her nose in the meeting going on tonight. Just ignore it."

"What if she calls Ford's cell and tips her that we're here before we're done?"

"Good point." Signaling to my Deputy at the door, I told him, "Find Treadway and let him know the status of the kitchen search then get outside and keep any bystanders, including the home owner, out."

"Roger Sheriff," the Deputy said and then was gone.

"I should have thought of that before," I said aloud, to no one in particular then I mentally slapped myself. Shaking my head to clear it, I put the two boxes of shotgun shells down and looked back in the ammo box. Under where the slugs had been was a box labeled for full metal jacketed .22 caliber rounds. I had the tech take a photo then I lifted that gently out, held it out for another photo then opened it.

"Bingo!" The box not only contained what it was supposed to, it was also missing a single round. I tipped it toward Shane and then toward Laura. She bagged and tagged the whole box.

"There are some loose, unjacketed .22 rounds in here along with the loose slug shells that were on top but no more jacketed .22s," I told Laura. "Go ahead and bag those other .22 cals too, just to be thorough."

Shane grinned, "Looks like we may have a case."

"Probably. It would really make me feel a lot better to find those binoculars too."

While Shane worked through the paperwork stacks in the den, I wandered back through the house. Treadway met me in the kitchen.

"Nothing more upstairs Sheriff and down here, other than the den, is mostly done too."

"Is there a basement Joe?"

"Already checked it. Just a ten by ten furnace room like most houses around here…too wet for much more."

"Let's head out to the garage then. We're still looking for binoculars, at a minimum."

Not even thinking, I stepped out the door from the kitchen into the driveway ahead of Treadway. The young deputy I'd sent outside minutes before was in place holding a half dozen residents with nothing better to do than gawk, at bay. When they saw me, they started shouting questions.

"Go on ahead Joe; I'll be right there."

I walked over to the deputy and the little crowd of people just a few steps from him. "Evening folks. I dipped my head in acknowledgement."

"What's going on Mel?" Molly, who'd called previously and left the message, now called out loudly, even though I could reach out and touch her from where I was standing.

"Now, now. This is a police matter. No one is hurt and

no one is under arrest. We're just looking into a few things. You folks need to back up off the lawn and let my people do their jobs.

No one moved. Politely, but in my best command voice, I admonished them, "That's not an option. All of you need to move back to no closer than the sidewalk now."

"We can't see nothin' from down there that far Sheriff," old man Purcell whined.

"Exactly," I replied and then urged them all back. I turned on one heel and headed for the garage.

In sharp contrast with the den, the garage was a neat and orderly. Tools hung on racks above old but scrubbed work benches along the back wall. A multi-drawer toolbox stood next to the row of work tables. Down both side walls were built in shelves that were lined with plastic tubs and totes, all neatly labeled and each with a matching lid. Fishing poles stood in a rack in one front corner and garden tools in a rack in the other.

Joe was working his way down the left side opening totes and peering inside. "Anything?" I asked him.

"What's on the label is what's in the tote, so far."

I started down the right side. I found summer jackets in a tote labeled summer jackets, and rock salt in a tote labeled that way. Quickly scanning down the rows of labels, I found a couple of totes labeled 'Hunting Clothes'. Playing on a hunch, I opened the first one. It was packed full of bright orange apparel. Opening the next, I found camouflage clothing but nothing else.

"We're in Terry Ford's domain Joe but I'm thinking Sheila wouldn't have wanted him to know she'd bought the binoculars. They're probably in a tote full of Christmas decorations or something." Frustrated already, I snapped the lids back on the tubs and replaced them.

"Or maybe she mixed it in with other similar stuff so, if he found them, she wanted him to think he'd just forgotten he had them, Sheriff." Joe drew my attention to the tote at his feet.

I checked the label, 'Hunting Gear'. Inside, among other hunting paraphernalia, were two sets of binoculars; one older in a case and one much newer in their original box.

CHAPTER 25

Denouement

Mama Rossi
Wednesday Evening, October 21st, 2014

Faye called to let us know she'd been asked to report to the Fall Festival meeting early to help set up coffee and snacks for the large group that was expected. Dana and I rode together, without her instead and arrived about 15 minutes early.

She pulled her car into the lot of the former school turned community center and parked to the left of a dark colored pick-up. Getting out on the passenger side, I only glanced at the truck at first, ensuring I didn't hit it with my door as I opened it.

As I made my way between the car and the truck, I glanced into the bed of the pick-up. My eye was caught by an old fashioned creel basket on the opposite side. I went around that way, reached over the side and hauled the basket up. Flipping open the lid, I peered inside and took a good look.

"Mama, what on earth are you doing?" Dana exclaimed.

"Nothing." I returned the creel to its former position.

"You can't just go around doing stuff like that, you know?"

Inside the community center, I immediately set about trying to corner Faye to tell her what I'd seen outside. Dana though was hell bent on interrupting me and pulling me in a different direction so all I could do was get Faye to promise to hear me out later.

After a few self-introductions to people Dana hadn't already met in one form or fashion and some pointed questions, we were directed to the gentleman in charge of the haunted house operation.

"Mama, this is Craig Stroud."

"You know him?" I asked my daughter.

"You look familiar," the man said to Dana, "but I just can't place you."

"We've never formally met. I'm Dana Rossi. I was with Mel during the, uh, incident at the Mushroom Festival back in the spring. I was in a wheelchair then."

"Ah yes, now I remember. An unfortunate incident that, but it seems that you're doing well."

"I'm fine and getting better every day. May I introduce my mother, Chloe Rossi?"

He extended his hand to my mother, "Mrs. Rossi, a pleasure."

Curious, I asked, "Whatever happened at the mushroom festival that was so unfortunate? Was someone poisoned?"

Craig lowered his voice, "In a manner of speaking, yes." At what I was sure was my look of utter disbelief he added, "It's not what you're thinking. It was nothing he ate at the festival. It turned out to be murder."

"I see," I said, but I really didn't and I didn't want to.

"So, what brings you ladies out tonight? Did you hear about all of this and decide you wanted to jump in and get involved?"

"As a matter of fact, yes," Dana told him. We took seats next to him and had a nice long chat about our haunt experiences and his needs while we waited for the formal meeting of the evening to kick off.

Faye joined us a couple of minutes before everything got started. By that time, Dana and Craig were deep in conversation and oblivious to us. Faye leaned toward me. "What did you want to tell me?" she whispered.

I looked around the now full cafeteria turned meeting hall. More than a hundred people milled about. I saw several faces that were already familiar to me in the crowd. "I can't say much here," I whispered back, but I found something pretty interesting outside in someone's truck."

"Who's truck? What did you find?" she fired back but quietly.

I leaned in closer and whispered to her.

Faye's jaw dropped as the President of the Festival Committee called the meeting to order.

After about a half hour of various reports and minor 'big picture' discussion, the meeting broke out into functional groups with everyone congregating in the group that met their primary interest to do specific final planning. Faye tugged me to join her with the food services group while Dana split off with Craig and his haunted house crew.

"Since you'll be back and forth during the next couple of weeks, you're not going to be much help to Craig's crew with the build anyway, right?"

"That's true, but I would still like to lend a hand with make-up and costuming. I'll make it a point to be here for the full festival."

Faye simply nodded and pulled me toward two tables place a little closer to the kitchen entrance and the snacks.

Each group quickly staked out a little territory in the large cafeteria, taking over a table or two. Some folks milled about too, not interested in any one specific focus but preferring to listen in for a few minutes on more than one or, I suspected, just there for the coffee and refreshments that were readily available near the food committee tables for the taking.

In our group, we'd been talking about set-up arrangements and scheduling needs for about ten minutes when the door from the main hallway swung open and Mel, in full uniform, one of her deputies and a man in a suit and tie strode in. My daughter-in-law scanned the room, her eyes finally coming to rest on the area where the decorating and staging committee was meeting.

She turned and said something in a low voice to the two men then, leaving them standing where they were, she made her way over to the decorating and staging group as all eyes in the room followed her. The only sound to be heard was the one Mel's service boot soles made as leather met tile while she walked.

Mel stopped behind the chair of Sheila Ford who looked up at her with an expression I could only describe as puzzled. "Mrs. Ford, I need to speak with you."

"Whatever for?" Sheila asked her.

"Could you come outside with me please and I'll

explain?"

"There's nothing you can say to me out there that you can't say to me right here. What's this all about? Is something wrong? What's happened now?"

"Sheila, please, you're not making this easy."

"Just tell me what it is you want me to know!" Sheila Ford's voice rose with each statement. Her tone was laced with fear.

Mel, the picture of calm, responded, "I'm sorry to have to do this like this; Sheila Ford, you're wanted for questioning. You're under arrest for the murder of Patricia Dunkirk and the attempted murder of your late husband, Terry Ford."

Mel hauled Sheila up out of her chair and continued to talk, presumably letting Sheila know her rights, but I could hear nothing above the bedlam that erupted in the room at the announcement of the charges. Almost everyone was out of their seat and they were all talking at once. The staid planning meeting had turned into total chaos.

Above it all, someone started screaming then switched to wailing. It was Sheila. The room reverberated with the sound of her cries and with the chatter of others.

Through the din, a man's voice rang out, calling for quiet. Even Sheila grew silent as we all looked toward the door for the source. The order had come from the uniformed deputy that had entered with Mel.

Mel's target wasn't hushed for long. She started right in on her, "You're crazy Mel. You've gone off the deep end. I didn't kill anybody! I don't even know that first person you named. You can't do this to me! Let me go! You have no reason to arrest me!" Sheila shouted on and on.

When Mel could get a word in, she tried to tell the shrieking woman, "I do have reason and the authorities in Tennessee will be extraditing you for questioning and likely arraignment on the charges within the next 24 hours, I can guarantee it."

"Tennessee? I haven't been to Tennessee in years! What are trying to pull here?"

I could sense Faye bristling beside me. Putting out a hand on her arm to steady her, I knew we were both recalling what Helen had told us at the funeral and Mel's revelation on the farm on Sunday. Everything seemed so long ago now but it was all coming back very quickly.

Dingy Dale got to his feet from within the circle of the decorating and staging group. He looked across at Sheila, "I just knew you were gunning for Terry! I never believed for a minute that he drowned out there without help."

"I didn't murder my husband Dale!"

"No, she didn't," Mel said, "but she did try once; didn't you Sheila?"

Sheila Ford dropped her head. Her reply of "I don't know what you're talking about," was barely audible, even in the now nearly quiet room. Everyone seemed to be hanging on every word.

"I think you do Mrs. Ford. There is a witness that knows you went to Tennessee the day Patricia Dunkirk, of Columbus, your husband's mistress, died. There's other evidence to prove you were there too."

"Did someone see me there?"

"No, they didn't have to. You cell phone, your purchases, and your fingerprints on a bullet casing and the weapon that shot the bullet will all prove your guilt."

"What…how…where…"

"Terry went to Tennessee to meet up with Patricia that weekend, didn't he Sheila?" She didn't respond but that didn't deter Mel. "You weren't too far behind him were you? You just needed to stop at Walmart in Pigeon Forge and buy a few things first, right?"

Sheila's face drained to a shade as pale as ash.

Mel must have picked up on it. I caught her as she hid a slight smile before she pressed on. "When Terry got down there, the woman was soaking in the Jacuzzi tub in their cabin. Terry must have decided to go outside for a smoke. He stood on the front balcony of their cabin, in front of the open door to the master bedroom, completely oblivious to you lying in wait on the hill across from him with binoculars, a rifle and a plan to kill him."

Ford swallowed hard but she said nothing.

Mel continued, "He must have moved just before your shot rang out. When he heard the shot and then Dunkirk cry out, and he realized what happened, he panicked. After finding her already dead by the time he got to her, he must have rinsed out the Jacuzzi and staged her body on the balcony, then cleaned the door handles and the tub again before leaving. He probably thought he hadn't touched anything but the wet tub and the door handles in the cabin in the short time he was there but he missed one piece of furniture that has since yielded his fingerprints. Regardless he left."

"What makes you so sure Terry didn't kill her…that woman? Maybe he wanted her dead!" Sheila Ford was obviously grasping for anything she could come by for her defense.

"I'll be honest Mrs. Ford, I had a hard time putting it all together without Terry to tell his side of the story. But the evidence doesn't lie. You intended to kill Terry that day. That's why you're being charged with attempted murder too. Quite frankly, Tennessee has a better chance than Ohio of making your murder charge for Dunkirk's death stick. It wasn't premeditated...hell, it probably was entirely an accident hitting and killing her, but an accidental death in the commission of a capital crime is still classified as a murder both here and there."

Mel started to lead Sheila Ford away but, before they reached the door, Dingy Dale called out, "What about Terry, Sheriff? Where's the charges for killing him? She had to have a hand in that, if she tried it before."

Mel handed Sheila off to the deputy and he led her out. She turned back into the room and addressed Dingy politely, "Mr. Walters, we're still looking into the death of Mr. Ford but, all indications are right now that his drowning was just an unfortunate accident. I'm sorry."

I cleared my throat and stood, "It was no accident at all, Sheriff," I called out from halfway across the room.

Faye stood up next to me, "She's right Mel. Oh, Terry did drown but someone was there when he did and just let him die. That person is right here in this room and it isn't Sheila Ford."

Chaos erupted again at Faye's pronouncement. Some people were shouting while others were looking around at their friends and neighbors wondering who might possibly have let a man die before their eyes. I watched as Mel and the man in the suit looked at each other in confusion.

Dana got up from her own group and walked over to us, fire in her eyes, "Mama, Faye; what you're talking about is called negligent homicide. It's a low level felony. You can't just make an accusation like that without evidence to back it up."

"Oh sweetie, we have evidence."

My daughter looked at me hard then said, "I think you two better spill whatever you have to Mel, and do it now, but don't say you haven't been warned."

I nudged Faye and, together, we moved a little closer to Mel. When I caught her attention again, I told her, "We have evidence Sheriff or, rather, it's readily available for you to see for yourself."

She nodded. "Go ahead then ladies, I'm listening." Around her, everyone else started to settle back down to listen in again. The true purpose of the meeting was all but forgotten.

Faye and I looked at each other again then I plunged in, "There are multiple people in this room that had it in for Terry Ford for one reason or another. Some of you didn't even bother with attending the man's funeral, your disdain for him was so great." I slowly walked around the room and first caught the eyes of Rich Johnson and his wife Amy in the finance committee group. I thought about saying something about them but the pained expression on Amy's face made me think twice. Enough damage had been done there. I moved on.

Just milling around was Art Majors. I caught his eye

too but he looked away quickly and went on about making himself a cup of coffee.

I moved around to the decorating committee grouping and looked right at Dale Walters.

He was unnerved and he jumped back up demanding, "Chloe, what on earth are you looking at me for?"

"You weren't upset when Terry died, were you Dale?"

Dale hesitated to answer for a long time but then, sighing, he opened up; "No…I…I wasn't."

A gasp rose in the room.

"But I didn't kill him! I wouldn't have let him drown! There's no way I could ever do anything like that."

"I didn't say you did Dale but I do think, perhaps you have a guilty conscience. You seem to hang around a bit in the area of Chuck's pond. Were you there the day Terry drowned? Did you see anything? Do you care to explain why you spend so much time in the area?"

"I do fish but I don't go to that pond to do it, if that's what you're asking. I'm not fond of blue gill at all and Chuck's pond is full of them. I certainly wasn't there they day Terry was there. For that matter, I didn't even know he was there." He looked a little scared and kept fidgeting. *Grown men shouldn't have any reason to fidget!*

I didn't respond; I just let him talk himself into a hole to fill in the awkward silence he'd created with his pause.

"Look Chloe…Faye…hell, Sheriff…it's not what you think. Those carvings, the carvings in my store…I tell everyone I do them but, actually, I don't. I even have my wife believing I just go out to the woods to be alone and carve." He turned to her and shot her a sheepish look. She pursed her lips and tried to control her emotions but her eyes shone with tears not yet ready to fall.

Dale sank back down in his chair and his shoulders slumped. "Honestly," he said, "I trade groceries, tobacco and other items, including a little company from time to time… to an old man that lives out there alone in exchange for them. He does them." He looked at his wife and then hung his head in shame.

I looked back at Faye. His confession wasn't what we had suspected and I felt bad for what my prodding at wrought out of him. Almost cowed into relenting, I glanced over and saw Art smirking by the coffee station. It was time to get the truth.

Again I looked at Faye. Her confirming nod gave me the strength I needed and I pressed on.

"Why the smirk Mr. Majors?" I called to him, mustering the firmest voice I could. Did you honestly think someone wouldn't figure it all out?"

"What on God's green earth are you talking about woman?" he queried me as he tried to intimidate me with his glare.

"Don't invoke the name of the Lord in front of a lie Mr. Majors. Tell us all, how long did you stand there that day watching Terry Ford drown?" Everyone in the room gasped again but I didn't let up on him. "How long Art? And, how many times did you go back to the scene of your crime? I know it was at least once because we were there one of those times." I pointed a finger between Faye and myself.

All eyes were on Art as his face reddened and he sputtered for a response.

"Come on Art, spill it. Did you push him in? Did you throw his bait in and laugh as he went after it? Did you steal that fishing reel you prized so much before or after he drowned?"

Majors lunged toward me. I backed up and then dodged but, before knew it Mel and the guy in the suit were wrestling with him.

After several long seconds that seemed like an eternity, he stopped struggling with them, stood straight, smoothed his shirt and spat at me, "You better watch who you're accusing of what!"

"Or what Art;" Faye questioned him, "what will happen to her?"

He spun to shoot Faye the same intense look he'd been favoring me with. "She doesn't know what she's talking about and neither do you. Yeah, I was out there the other day. I fish out there a lot; ain't that right Chuck?" He scanned the finance grouping looking for Chuck Knox.

Chuck shook his head and said, "This is your fight Art. Why don't you tell us all the truth?"

"I got nothin' to say to any of you people. I'm out of here."

"Whoa, not so fast buddy." Mel put a hand out to stop him and the suited man with her jumped into his path. "Let's hear them out and hear your side."

"There's no 'side' Sheriff. They don't have any proof of anything because I didn't do anything! Terry drowned. Everyone knows he couldn't swim!"

Gathering my courage, I stepped over closer to him and looked him in the eye. "All the proof anyone needs that you were present at his death is in the back of your truck, Art."

"What do you have in your truck, Mr. Majors?" Mel asked him.

"I...I don't know...my fishing gear probably is all. Nothing like what she's implying!"

"*Your* fishing gear?" I fired back. "Don't you mean the creel basket that belonged to Terry Ford with the Abu Garcia fishing reel in it that you so coveted but he wouldn't sell you? Were you so mad at Terry over the lost RV deal that, when he decided not to sell you the reel after all, you went over the edge? When you saw that reel in his basket out there that day, did it make you crazy?"

The veins in Art's neck bulged, "That reel should have been mine all along!" he bellowed.

I have him! Everyone in the room looked startled but Faye and Mel. Mel moved to take Majors' arm. Her sidekick quickly recovered when she turned to him, addressed him as Shane, and asked for his cuffs.

"You're not cuffing me! I didn't kill him. The dumb bastard went into the water to unsnag his line. He must have got out too far and got stuck or slipped or something. I don't know! I didn't stick around to find out. I admit I took the creel with the reel in it and I left. He was alive when I left; I swear!"

Primed now, I went for the jugular; "Is that really what happened? You *just said* 'everyone knows he couldn't swim'. Did he actually go into the water to retrieve the bait tub you threw in or did you throw it in the direction of the deeper part of the pond while he was out there?"

"That's the second time you've brought up bait! I didn't

see any bait!"

Faye spoke up, "Nobody fishes without bait Art. Everyone knows *that*."

I looked at Mel and Shane but said loud enough for everyone in the room to hear, "The lid to the bait tub marked with that day's date in black Sharpie is in the creel but there was no bait to be found out there." In a softer voice, for only Mel and Shane to hear, I said, "The creel is in the bed of his pickup out in the lot beside Dana's car."

"You have the right to remain silent," Mel recited as she cuffed him.

* * *

Mama Rossi
Late Wednesday Evening, October 21st, 2014
The Boar's Head Bar

After the raucous community meeting turned fiasco, we all decided we needed a drink. Faye, Dana and I headed to the Boar's Head.

The place wasn't crowded which was what we'd hoped for on a Wednesday night. Barb happened to be there and she greeted us herself.

"Celebrating something ladies?" she asked.

Dana, smiling, answered her, "My mom and Faye just caused a little dust up at the community meeting and now they're parched. After sitting through that whole scene, we thought maybe we could all use a little adult refreshment."

"Will Mel and Jesse be along?" Barb looked between Faye and me for confirmation.

"Jesse's probably already in bed," Faye said, rolling her eyes.

"That's probably a 'no' on Mel too. I texted her and invited her of course, but she's the one that's got to deal with the aftermath of the whole shooting match. She may be at the station for quite a while tonight," Dana told Barb. Dana's face was clearly pained at the thought of what Mel must be trying to sort through.

"Let me get you all your drinks and then I think you better fill me in." Barb hustled back to the bar and reappeared rather quickly.

We spent the next half hour recounting all of both stories for Barb then we passed another half hour, as a group, working out a plan for me to make it back to work at the Fall Festival - if they would still have me after the negative sensation I'd caused tonight – and to work on decorating her new home. It was all shaping up to be an interesting holiday season.

About the Author

Anne Hagan is an East Central Ohio based government employee by day and author by night. She, her wife and their dogs live in a tiny town that's even smaller than the Morelville of her first fiction series and they wouldn't have it any other way. Anne's wife grew up there and has always considered it home. Though it's an ultra-conservative rural community, they're surrounded there by family, longtime friends and many other wonderful people with open hearts and minds. They enjoy spending time with Anne's son, with their nieces and nephews and doing many of the things you've read about in this book or that will be 'fictitiously' incorporated into future Morelville Mystery Series books. If you've read about a hobby or a sport here, they probably enjoy doing it themselves or someone very close to them does.

Viva Mama Rossi! is the fifth book in the Morelville Mysteries series by Anne. If you enjoyed this one, please check out the other books in the series, ***Relic***, ***Busy Bees***, ***Dana's Dilemma*** and ***Hitched and Tied*** to see where it all began for private investigator Dana Rossi and Sheriff Melissa 'Mel' Crane. These mysteries stand-alone but they're certainly better together.

Please watch for the future continuation of this series and for an all new cozy mystery series, coming soon by Anne.

Also Written by the Author

Relic: The Morelville Mysteries – Book 1 – The first Dana and Sheriff Mel mystery!

Busy Bees: The Morelville Mysteries – Book 2 – Murder, mayhem and a little bit of romance continue the series.

Dana's Dilemma: The Morelville Mysteries – Book 3 – The relationship matures between Mel and Dana in an installment that features a breaking Amish character, an ex-girlfriend, a conniving politician and murder.

Hitched and Tied: The Morelville Mysteries – Book 4 – Mel and Dana attempt to bring their growing relationship full circle but family, duty and family duties all conspire to get in the way.

Please Leave a Review

If you've enjoyed this book, please tell your friends about it. Did you know that you can lend the book? To do so, simply follow the instructions Amazon provides for loaning a book. Meanwhile, if you have a chance, I would really appreciate an honest review on Amazon. You can review this book by following this link: **Viva Mama Rossi! Review Page**. Thank you!

Check Anne Out on her blog, on Facebook or on Twitter:

For the latest information about upcoming releases, other projects, sample chapters and everything personal, check out Anne's **blog** at https://AnneHaganAuthor.com/ or like Anne on **Facebook** at https://www.facebook.com/AuthorAnneHagan. You can also connect with Anne on **Twitter** @AuthorAnneHagan.

Made in the USA
Middletown, DE
08 November 2015